Maura Quell

Maura Quell

by

Rita Donovan

BuschekBooks
Ottawa

Copyright © 2013 Rita Donovan
All rights reserved.

Library and Archives Canada Cataloguing in Publication

Donovan, Rita, 1955-
   Maura Quell / Rita Donovan.

ISBN 978-1-894543-75-0

   I. Title.

PS8557.O58M39 2012   C813'.54   C2012-906170-0

Cover image: cover photograph by Anna Maria Carlevaris

Printed in Winnipeg, Manitoba, by Hignell Book Printing.

BuschekBooks
P.O. Box 74053
5 Beechwood Avenue
Ottawa, Ontario, Canada K1M 2H9
www.buschekbooks.com

For John Leonard Donovan, Anna Carlevaris and David Taylor,

Three beloved, who have all gone travelling.

On March 23, 1810, the converted warship *Canada* sailed to New South Wales on her second voyage, carrying prisoners bound for "Transport Beyond the Seas." The ship existed. The prisoners existed. But the characters in this story, and in the parallel story line, are fictional.

It all comes back to me, over me, quite like a dream, a night song she'd sing to me before I fell all the way down to sleep. She'd lift her arm, the sleeve rolled, and it would brush across my face as her hand reached for my forehead. I'd try not to flinch or turn away at the rough, dry weight of it. It was she, comforting, and I wanted the touch.

I will be on the boat, they say. I'll be going to Transport. It's that or hanging; they screw up their faces. Better than burning. That or the rope for you, Maura Quell. They laugh at me. O my darling, they say. The short leap into long ago.

Death on the gallows. And they whisper to me the worst of it. The surgeons. My Maker, spare me from the public cutting up, all the people looking on my spare body as they rend me…. No.

I will get the Transport. They tell me it's down to me to take care as there's no one, there is not one of them will look after me on that hulk. The creatures in the pit will be there, shrieking and screeching, their sores and their smells swirling in the hold.

Say farewell to this sweet soil, O my girl. So says he. To torment me, his job in this fine place. Sweet soil? Sweet it has not been, no softness here as a body would know. Can the colony be any worse than this prison? He says I am young; I might survive it. I'll end up a broken vessel, says he. So bid farewell, O my girl.

And I must.

I know this much. Of the people who leave, hardly any come back.

Inasmuch as she has come of decent people and befitting her age and general condition, Maura Quell will be held until such time as Transport is arranged, for a period of seven years....

This is what they tell me. This is how they will say it.

In seven years I shall be twenty. Another person will answer to my name, a woman hard and used, a vessel chipped and damaged.

So I must say farewell to this, my life, my only, very, life.

I am Maura Quell. I come from Epping, late of London gutters. I had a mother. Didn't we all have a mother, anyway? She died in a chair by the door. I think, perhaps, she starved. She was talking one moment, and she went quiet; I thought she was sleeping. She used to sleep on the chair when I had the space by the fire. I left her there for a time so she could rest.

I had a brother, Eugene. He was with me for a time and then I lost him. It was on the streets, and I looked for him for a long time after, in the alleyways, on the grates, in the troughs and by the burning barrels. I never did find him. He was little, just four or so when I had him there. He couldn't keep up on those legs.

I would like to say farewell to the trees out back. They come in my dreams so I know they are real. There, outside the window and I could see them over her shoulder when she put me in the bed, Eugene just a babe by my side. Before the city, in the small years when we were all together.

There is also a bird I would like to note. Here and now, it seems strange, for I wouldn't be able to tell you which it was if I saw it once again. But one twilight when I was sore and cold after looking for the boy, the sun was going down behind the dark rooftop and I walked the cobbles and saw, perched on the edge of a fence post, this glowing bird. A robin? Too tiny, and he was as alone as I was. He picked his way along the fence, just to let me know the way it's done, and he stared into me with his black beetle eyes and rose up over the sleeping man, the factory and the roof. It was the last day I looked for

Eugene and I felt that, perhaps, the bird was telling me something, though I didn't know what it might be.

I should have more, more to depart from. But how can you take leave of what you don't know, or learn to let go of what you don't have?

I should like to say farewell to the little cottage by the water. It would have a hearth, and walls that would stand forever, for my grandchildren to play within. Goodbye, then, to the tall roses, the day lilies, the hollyhocks by the door. Mint, the healing mint, the clean smell of mother's hand.

So, too, should I release the young man from his obligation. I would have met you soon, I expect. You'd be delivering out back with your horse and cart; you'd carry in the victuals, the grains and the wood. I would see you there and smile at you.

Maura Quell, you'd say. What kind of a girl is Maura Quell?

Well, she is exactly what she wants to be and no less. And who would be asking the question so boldly, and with my name already on his lips?

You would stammer then, or you would not. Perhaps you'd look me in the eye like you've done it more than once and say, Timothy Ellis, or you'd say Jamie Norton.

Lyall Norgate.

Missus.

Goodbye to the pressure of your face next to mine.

The guard is on his way. I can hear the curses. He says I'll have no worries, that I'll be the snug harbour of a prison man or a ship's mate.

Farewell to the cambray shirt, the linen waistcoat embroidered in peonies and leaves.

I am finished, says he. Complete? Like the stitch-work on the sleeve of a fine, fine garment? Done like the daylight, is what he really means.

9

The Lord Mayor of London. The Recorder.

"That's the Sergeant-at-Arms, that one," hisses Hettie Rags Crenshaw. "Look, there's his mace."

Others we cannot fathom.

"Who's he? He scares me."

"Sheriff of London."

Jury coming in, taking the oath, faces like the dough rising round bakery road. They move into the wooden jury box and are penned.

O, Maura Quell, how are you here, anyway? And wouldn't Mother stand, wouldn't she put her sweet body here, in front, before the terrible glare of the Sheriff?

A cold air comes in and fills up my garments. The Mayor, the Sheriff, the Recorder, all in heavy robes. Do they feel this urgent frost at the tips of the fingers? It is a dust, not unlike coal dust from the colliery dockside. But finer, lighter, a dust of the air, a haze. Holding me, keeping me from falling over.

"Maura Quell, you are indicted on the double felony charge of robbery, to wit, on 4 February 1809 did take one cambray shirt, value 3 s., from the shop of John Butler, proprietor."

Maura, Maura, where you got to, girl? Weaving through the field behind the house, grass tickling legs, now knees.

"How do you plead?"

Caught in a mouse hole, stumbling forward, arms out, hands in clover.

"M'Lord...."

And it is so soft.

"M'Lord...I don't understand. Double? For I took but one...."

"So you admit you stole?"

Perfume, this clover, but the bees arrive.

"Are you sound, girl? Answer me!"

Icy air; the courtroom throbs, a finger with a splinter.

"I took but one thing, Sir. I...was hungry."

"So did see fit to rob a decent citizen of his property? And a double felony, girl, signifies a capital offense, which you have admitted to committing."

The dough faces turn, look at me. Do any of them have girls at home? No. Not girls like Maura Quell.

The haze in the air is lifting. The face of the Recorder tightens. I see the glint on the sword blade behind him, and even on the forehead of the Sergeant-at-Arms.

"Maura Quell."

"Look, she's swaying already from the heave of the ship," a voice hangs in the splintering air.

"You have been found guilty of robbery and have been hereby sentenced to Transport beyond the seas for a period of seven years."

Thus go the Assizes. Thus goes my life.

I am with the women gone.

In the dream Eugene is tumbling in clover, his legs wrapped in the clinging green. Mother is bright, with the sun behind her.

O, Maura, what have you got up to? Look, your fingers are red. The berries were for later, you silly, silly girl.

But she smiles all the while and Eugene shrieks with delight. I looked for him on the streets, crying in the open air. Went past a pair of stairs and another pair of stairs, walked the length and breadth, down Fish Street Hill, over to Blue Anchor Yard, Virginia Street.... And I called out to him, I cried his name to the edges of the buildings. The rats heard me. The dogs heard me. The man with the strong arms and the scar heard me, and then no one heard the screaming when he took me. I tasted his blood and then it was him bellowing and all of London seemed to come running. But he also ran, and left me standing in my torn frock, my arms wrapped round me, my brother still gone.

Take care of Eugene. Wasn't it the only command she had ever given me? I was but a child myself, yet I knew that this might be the most important thing. *Maura,* she said, *you watch out for your brother and you stay together.*

Then she went to sleep in the chair. I had to pull Eugene from her lap. I had to slap his hands until he cried. And then we cried, the two of us, while the sun went down out the doorway, and the light along the path slid away.

11

O Maura, my girl. You were come of decent people.

I had a friend, Mary Lavender. We'd play jumping games, always laughing. Her old man was gone and her mum took in travellers and cleaned for her betters. Mary Lavender wanted to read as well, so we sat together at the table and went through verses from the Bible. Mary was going to the city soon, and I would miss her. I thought that I'd never leave the cottage. But then Father was gone as well, an accident, they called it, though my mother swore as I had never heard and she spit in the doorway at the man as he left.

The cottage tree. The green glass bottle in the window. The smell of mint.

And mother in the chair, sitting up all night so that we could sleep closer to the fire, Eugene's little body like a flower curled in the twilight. So easy to wrap him in the blanket, to fit it round his shoulders.

Is he covered where he is now? Did anybody cover him up?

"So you'll be in with us, then," says Hettie Rags Crenshaw. "I'll be needing a servant on board that hulk."

"You, a servant?" says another, with a whoop. "Well, I never."

Bessie Harclough is sick again. They can't send her like this, though perhaps she'll be delivered by the time the ship makes sail. Bessie's mind is playing with her. She whispers that it was her employer that was the cause of it, creeping in like a night breeze, and then turning her out when she came to him in need.

I see how it is. I'm not a child, as they think and imagine. The hands in the street travelled all over me and, but for my great shout, I too might be stuck up on the stone slab, moaning for Jesus Christ to take my misery away.

Strange. She is with a child unwanted, while Eugene.... He had no garments worth stealing and so would not have served the needs of Cassie Jukes, who is sentenced to Transport for stealing children just to take their clothes.

"What happens to the children after?" I heard somebody ask. I listened over at the rim of their voices.

"What?" says she. "Not my doin'," says she. "All I wants is their linen pinnies."

And the child, the infant, what of it then? Naked in London, a child, a baby.

"Not my doin'."

Eugene had nothing worth taking, his boots barely holding at the seams, his shirt, and stained trousers torn at the knee. The patch was flapping. I meant to put a needle to it, but first I had to find a needle.

If I thought that Cassie Jukes had ever been near him I would take her ginger head and beat it against the stones of this wall until her eyes rolled, insensible, and she stopped saying not my doin'. I would splinter her bones and leave them for the calciner.

She picks her teeth with her filthy nail.

I would deliver her body to the anatomists and her scrawny limbs would be dissected and that smile would disappear.

One grey crape gown
One green Coventry gown
One black coat
Three linen aprons

We are here for our crimes. But the lice, what crimes have they committed? For they far outnumber us in this stinking place. This is the Common Side of Newgate. I know the other side is better, but it takes coin I have not got.

I am watching a girl. She speaks to no one. Taller than I am, her hair like a dark halo around her head. She is called Caroline Lockett, they tell me. She stands more than she sits, over by the window that opens on to the inside wall of the prison. She cannot see anything, but there is nothing to see. And she speaks to no one at all.

"Is she mute?" I ask one of the old ones, who opens her gums and coughs in my face. Then she waggles a crooked finger in the girl's direction and says, "Nobody's got a word out of her. She's simple, that one is."

But I have been watching her. There is little else to do. Her name, if it is correct, is certainly grand enough. Her bearing is not, yet she doesn't stoop like some. Her clothes hang off her frame, but that is her age, like mine. The fabric was once fine, and the weave even and finished.

She could be mute. But she is not simple. She stays away from the likes of Hettie Rags Crenshaw, for one. She shifts away from wickedness and confrontation, curling up on the farthest, coldest slab.

I should like to speak to her, but it means getting past the old ones and the others. The one who pulled my hair until a clump of it came away. The one who reached out when I passed and took hold of my person in a disgusting manner.

Caroline Lockett, would you meet me by the far wall? Will you look this way and see all of these words in my eyes? Caroline Lockett, you remind me of someone else. Of Mary Lavender. You bring to mind so many, many things. Now my eyes are stinging. Pinpricks. A rush of warmth. There, now, what am I to do now?

I have given Caroline Lockett her own history. I watch as she walks by the far wall. They let her be; they think she is cursed. I almost laugh at this, but they think her the bearer of bad fortune. You foolish women, look where you are!

Yet I would like to be so named. For they would leave me alone. They curse around me, and come to blows at times. They pursue me, coax me, slap me and sometimes attempt more. I am quick and agile. I move and speak and play them against one another. I can tell which are true, which are souls like myself that have found themselves here by a stroke of fate. And I can tell the others, those who would have ended here or on the gallows no matter what.

Maura Quell, don't you be getting yourself mixed up with the likes of them.

No, Mother.

Caroline Lockett, her name is, or shall be. Caroline Lockett, you are of the same age as Maura Quell. Caroline has a home and perhaps both mother and father who are moving heaven and earth to get her sentence lifted. They will speak to solicitors, Attorneys will be sought and paid for. Look at the weave on her dress; is that not a garment of onetime quality?

Caroline Lockett will have a solicitor on her behalf. Her mother is even now folding and tucking silk underthings in a cloth bag to carry to the prison. The cook is preparing a portable feast, a grand affair. Jellied pork, cold chicken, salad greens, aspic, those things Eugene used to see in the windows and cry for. Well, cry no more, for Caroline will have them all. They will be brought in past Ludgate Hill and Holborn, right into Newgate itself, carried in by servers in crisp white garments. The servers will open the cell door, trample over the clot of women in the way, and set a table over on the stone slab where Caroline sleeps. Candlesticks will be cold to the touch, the silver ornate. But the flame, the flame will have us unclenching our fists, warming our hands, which will be clean and sweet-smelling.

Caroline will lift up her strong, unbowed head, smile at her servants, and with the briefest nod at Maura Quell, invite her to the candlelit repast.

They've told her it's the hobbies that will save her. She will be salvaged, that is, by the same sort of activity that keeps fidgety preschoolers focussed until they toddle off for nappy nap.

Salvaged but not saved, for there is no saving Aris Sandall. Look at her: forty-nine, living in a by-all-accounts generous one-bedroom walk-up with last year's Christmas lights dangling outside the front window. Chip, chip, the colour flakes off every time a breeze taps the bulb against her pane.

Dr. Grogan thinks she's well into the mid-life blues phase, the phenomenon other, better-trained physicians call menopause. But her cheerful doctor thinks it's just that generalized feeling of being lost in the middle of your life.

Like Hansel and Gretel in the woods? Theseus in the labyrinth? There did the good doctor study?

"Now, look. I could tell you to join lawn-bowling, but that would be patronizing."

So instead he advises her to find her "passion," a hobby or interest that will lift her sails. He talks like that, inflating metaphors at the dock only to have them hit the doldrums out at sea.

"It's not for me to decide," he says.

And he's right. He is not Aris Sandall; more's the pity, as he could do with a little humiliation and anonymity.

And as for her passion, well, her passion might well be illegal for all anyone knows. She can hear the insanists out there cheering as they power up their chainsaws.

There it is, the disdain.

"You don't get through life like that," says Dr. Grogan.

Well, you do. But you disdain the process. You graffiti the door on the way out.

Yet, for all of it, she is not about to knuckle under. The years have made her almost impervious to the idiots on the bus:

Baseball cap:	"Ketchup or hot sauce?"
Foot on seat:	"Ketchup."
Cap:	"Virgins or hookers?"
Foot:	"Hookers."
Cap:	"Behind the goal or the bench?"
Foot:	"Bench."

"So, a glass half-empty kind of person," the doctor nods.

"Glass of what?" Aris says, as he jots in her file.

She needs to do something in the after-hours, those moments she is not going to, surviving at, or returning from, work.

She writes copy. She writes for inanimate objects. Pacemakers. Defibrillators. Assist pumps. Artificial hearts.

This is one of those days. Her cubicle is almost near a window, which doesn't open. Safety-measure, to keep the employees inside. On her desk is a barometer shaped like a golf club, Secret Santa having confused her with the temp who was on contract last winter.

There is room for a plant, by why do that to a plant? On the furry, oatmeal-upholstered 'wall' she has tacked a picture of the Rose Bowl Parade, with the highlighted text beneath it noting the hundreds of thousands of roses that have been "snipped" for the day. Miss California has a rose tiara. Are those women wearing flower bustiers? Ouch! People wave from undoubtedly fragrant floats, caught for posterity in their own funeral procession.

Now, now. What would Dr. Grogan say? Something about glasses. And emptiness.

You must take certain precautions to ensure that your new pacemaker functions correctly. Blahblahblah most appliances currently in the home will not significantly affect the operation of your pacemaker. But it is important to note that machinery used in power-generating, or utilizing a strong magnetic pull, may interfere with the blahblahblah optimal performance of your pacemaker.

Hmmmm….. Bugs Bunny's giant magnet from the ACME company comes to mind.

Advanced technology may cause future models of cell phones to interfere significantly with your pacemaker. Research continues in this field.

What kind of research? 'Go ahead, Joey, see if we can blow up Uncle Dave!'

She ploughs through these thick and tangled fields looking for a way to embellish. She thinks of the people who will be reading this copy, people who have had life-altering surgeries, who have fallen to the floor in department stores. People who have made wills. She wants to make it lighter, more human. But how?

It is possible in rare cases that certain home devices such as heating pads or TV remotes could interfere with the running of your pacemaker, on occasion causing it to miss a beat. But this generally does not occur.

Dear Borg Person,

By now you know that some things don't work. Might be your heart. Might be our product. Ironically, "that's life." So get out there and enjoy the symphony. Take that second scoop of ice cream. Golf, you bastard, golf.

It is a Friday off for Aris Sandall. She normally wastes these flex-time days on laundry and groceries, but today she has pulled on a sweater and skirt, choked down something multigrain and phoned for the unfamiliar bus route.

Mints? No. They make her thirsty.

Gum? Noisy, and inappropriate given the setting.

The door is massive; leaded glass panes. Aris pulls and feels both her strength and the lack of it before the portal finally inhales and sucks her in.

Is the architecture designed to make her feel small, or to make her sense the enormity of the knowledge, of the task at hand? It works, whatever its intent, because she feels out of proportion here.

She waits in line to be registered, "processed," the clerk verifying her identity, her address, her contact information.

"Photo ID?"

She doesn't drive. Her passport is in the safety-deposit box at the bank. And her health card is one of the old ones, without a picture.

"I'll need something else….SIN card?"

She doesn't like giving out her social insurance number.

"Look, all I want to do is look something up. I'm…interested in genealogy. I just want to poke around…."

Apparently, poking around is not the official term for scholarly endeavour. Aris proffers her SIN card and the clerk grudgingly and wordlessly sticks an identi-card into a plastic sleeve on a string and passes it to her.

Aris Sandall. A temporary library card number.

She is to wear her plastic at all times.

The clerk points a long finger in the direction of the lockers.

Derek always said she had her head in the clouds. He said that Aris closed the main road while she swept off the pathways.

Their marriage failed because of this lack of communication.

What was wrong with the pathway, with being, if you will, less Stalag about things? Besides, she wasn't that disorganized after all. She wrote copy, didn't she?

A word about restenosis. For patients who have been given a procedure in which stents have been inserted into blood vessels, there is a possibility of scarring. In a small minority of cases this scarring can lead to a repetition of the initial closing of....

Oh, bloody good.

But Aris knows that it isn't about being disorganized. The fact is, Derek's aversion to the interesting pathways had sent him down the main, well-travelled road to Alice, the input clerk, and Sidney, the condo board rep. And Aris knows that, organized or not, she still possesses the GICs and the rental property she got in the divorce settlement eight years ago.

The elevator doors slide open. She enters a high-ceilinged room with medium-dark wood panelling and surrounding shelves of reference books. One wall is floor-to-ceiling windows, facing out onto a green and wavy world.

It doesn't look that verdant from the outside, Aris muses. The grass is always greener...and it occurs to her that someone created the phrase in a moment just like this one, with the silver light framing the trees outside. Maybe that is what genealogy is like, finding those nods across time and space.

Long, gleaming tables invite her. Only three other patrons dot the large room.

Groaning boards, that's what they look like. Banquet tables of old, Henry VIII at the far one, making a pig of himself, a future heart patient?

Your ventricular device (VAD), while not replacing your heart, will help pump blood if your ventricle is failing.

There is one person being served at the Reference Desk so Aris settles at the end of the table in front of the counter. Odd-looking gentleman at the desk, one of those career-bachelor types, though not by choice. Wool vest, shirt and tie. Glasses. When he looks up the light glints off the spectacles and he looks eyeless. Moon-faced.

The client in front of Aris has a ream of paper clutched to her chest. Damn her. Probably an entire family tree to climb. Look at those hips. All of her ancestors had those child-bearing hips, her family tree probably gigantic.

That's it, yes, point to those large volumes along the wall. Give her a microfilm.

Of course she drops her file cards. One flips under the reference desk. Probably the lynchpin, the ancestor who holds the tree together. Have fun working it out without great-great Uncle Morris.

The woman heads over to the other end of the reading room. Aris hops up. She has a piece of blank paper and her mandatory pencil.

His name is Dunstan. Dunstan Regimbald, the moon-faced man. He says he will help her design a methodology, give her starting points, show her how to work the machines. He steps from behind the desk and she can see she is not incorrect in assuming he is a bachelor. He has bachelor trousers, the telltale sign of neglected grey flannel. The shirt is permanent press, the shoes are black Reeboks, not real shoes.

"So, if you'd like to let me know what it is you have so far?"

Aris stares.

"In your research. You have a name, of course, and do you have a date?"

She hasn't had a date in years.

"Do you know where I might begin?" she asks.

She supposes she could begin by untwisting his collar. The man is bordering on unkempt. How old is he? Thirty-five; thirty-nine?

"I have very little," she adds.

Dr. Grogan is cringing. *Be positive.*

"She...I think she might be a long lost relative. I just remember her name, growing up. My grandmother used to talk about her. Said she was a prisoner long ago. She used to say it to scare me into putting away my coloured pencils." Why is she saying this? Why is she showing the moon-faced one her sad, sterile memory?

"I see."

"You do?"

Now it is his turn to do the stammer dance.

"Yes. That is, many people come in with little more than a desire to follow a mystery around for a while. I'll give you a paper to fill out. Perhaps the questions will jar some memories."

He disappears behind the counter and returns with a single sheet. Aris scans it.

City or Port of departure? Date of departure? Country of immigration? Other family information…. Aris nods her way down the page. She carefully prints the name at the top, under "Ancestor," and hands the sheet back to Dunstan Regimbald.

"Hmmmm…. 'Maura Quell.' Okay. So. The world is our oyster."

Another glass half-full type.

There's a ship that sailed last August. The *Indispensable*. Cassie Jukes had a cousin aboard, a murderess, she is fond of repeating. There is talk among the women—one of them heard the guards—that we will be taken soon to board a ship.

It is strange to think of stepping away from land. The world of late has been dark alleys and dusty lanes. And now, here, where I reach out in either direction and touch another filthy body.

I woke up near dawn and that's when I saw her, Caroline Lockett, perched above the slop bucket, her dress hiked, her face drawn even as blood stained down her white leg. She did not know I saw her. I squinted my eyes closed just as she pulled the dress to cover her. When I peeked again she was back on the slab. She is down at the end with the bucket. It's unbearable, but there they leave her alone. I try to tell myself that this is the good outcome of my conviction. I remind myself of the other possibilities. Nettie Crenshaw has seen women hanged and burned. When she was just a girl, herself, she saw Margaret Sullivan go. Back in '86, she says.

"Always went to Tyburn Fair, me."

She says it's the bell she remembers.

"The Execution Bell, they call it. Right. They says to Margaret, they says the prayer:

>"*All you that in the condemned hole do lie,*
>*Prepare you, for tomorrow you shall die.*
>*Watch all, and pray: the hour is drawing near*

That you before the Almighty must appear.
Examine well yourselves, in time repent.
That you may not to eternal flames be sent;
And when St. Sepulchre's Bell in the morning tolls,
The Lord above have mercy on your souls...."

The women laugh, but it is a wary laugh.

And then Margaret, in her white garment, looking from a distance like a schoolgirl, stands up on the stool for her punishment.

Yes, ma'am, I have talked out of turn instead of doing my lessons. And the faggots pile higher.

Nettie plays it out. She likes this tale. She likes telling of the Bell of St. Sepulchre, the tolling in the head of Margaret Sullivan. And Margaret, what was she thinking as she heard the passing bell, the bell of death? What did she know of twigs and sticks and the way they burn so prettily?

Nettie Rags Crenshaw has tales of hangings, spectacles such as have them agog.

"Some call it Nevergreen," the gallows from which they hang.

"They call it the morning drop. And those that are hanged they say dance upon the air."

I shivered, then, when she said that. I would not like to dance upon nothing. I fear stepping away from the land.

Caroline Lockett was listening as well and I saw her stiffen her shoulders when she heard. She is not simple, not by a long way.

So I am resolved that this is the best outcome of the situation. There is no choice, for I have no one to plead for me, no last attempt to release me from Transport. In my history of Caroline Lockett her parents are working frantically to gain an audience and state their case. You have only to look at her, M'Lord, to know that she is not like these common thieves. There was a misunderstanding at best, M'Lord. She is of good stock.

Ah, but she has cramps today and is all alone. The women are in clusters around Bessie Harclough, who is in distress. It is my chance.

It is actually colder here, in this end of the cell than up where I am. She's lying with her knees drawn and she looks smaller as I get closer. I am confused by it—she gets smaller?

Her eyes are closed; her lips are tight.

"Sometimes it helps to get up and walk," I whisper. This is new to me as well, this bending over. "You know, good to keep moving."

She does not open her eyes. I know she's awake because I can see ideas flitting across her lids.

"I'm Maura. Maura Quell."

Do they open at all? A slit, enough to take me in? Eyes can do that, take in everything even as they are only just cracked open. Is it a nod from Caroline Lockett? The tiniest tip of her head?

Bessie Harclough screams then, and the women yell for the guard, and I go back to the other end and watch what happens then.

Bessie Harclough is dead. So says the guard. Her brat as well, and now there is nothing to wonder except whether her body will be sent to the surgeons for dissection.

"An' there she was, luv, spread open like a treacle tart."

Bessie Harclough will not be on the ship. She will not nurse her babe on deck on her way to the end of the world.

Caroline Lockett came over to me, near me, when the food was brought. She got up from her side and, bold as brass, picked her way over to where I was crouched close to the door. She said nothing, as always, and her glance was to my feet, not my face, but it was clear, it was clear she was coming to me. We ate like that, side by side. I saw that her foot was infected. Something scabbing it along the ankle.

She has delicate wrists, holding the bowl, and she has this… this presence. It's strange. It's like she's a ghost, except she's not a ghost. She's here, but she's haunting.

Perhaps it's her silence, but she turns my mind toward her, and she makes the noise, the drone, go away. I do not feel this at any other time, not since Eugene. Nor do I trust it, for did I not lose the boy? Did he not slip away, his round cheeks and watery blue eyes, his face cupped in my hand, curly head in the crook of my elbow, and then nothing?

I would like to wash. To be clean, sitting there beside her. We are, all of us, filthy. But I would wash, clean myself. I would brush my hair with that fine silver and brocade hairbrush on Missus' night table, she who turned me in.

It is so cold. This is the worst of it, I think, the cold. Fingers no longer reach out and feel anything. A rod of ice rests in the spine, dulling everything except the original pang, preserving it there and making us stand like frozen sentinels. Legs tingle but feet are gone, replaced by heavy lumps of tree root that must be dragged forward step by step.

The breast, the heart, is stilled, its patter no more than a flutter, the stirring of a leaf.

Bessie Harclough and her babe. Two leaves, two still and silent leaves.

If I'd a needle, I'd have stitched her hem.

We're to be taken to a lighter and by lighter out to the ship. Where is the family of Caroline Lockett, who will burst in with news of her pardon? Where is the hamper of bread, the bandage for her ankle?

I am sorry, Caroline, sorry they have not come for you. My fondest, fondest thoughts go into this unfolding, but it seems not to be, as though our prayers are trapped within the stone walls, just as we are, whispering up there, above our heads.

"Oy, look at them two, up to all sorts. Why dontcha come 'ere and give us a tickle?"

My shoe is broken or I would kick out at her. She is rank and her teeth rot in her head. I move closer to Caroline Lockett as we walk the edges.

"I...know you don't speak. Mother always said I speak enough for two...I'm Maura."

I hold out my hand, which no one would ever want to touch. She looks down at it passively, her eyes behind her eyes. She looks at it as if my hand were a fish washed up dockside.

It is between us. I turn it over and hold it open. Something jitters in her face and I see the spark of a smile. My eyes play tricks perhaps it is merely a twitch. But she moves her shoulder closer to mine as we make our rounds. Her ankle looks bad, what I can make out of it. I know a plant leaf that would ease the itching. It grew out back; I remember mother picking it when I was stung that time. Mother handing it to me, telling me to rub it on the spot. The leaf firm, sure in my fingers, grass warm on the legs as the wind blew through. On the way back, an unmended pot by the side of the path, with a bird's nest tucked inside.

Caroline's hands quite as bad as my own. Had those fingers ever worn rings, been adorned, the nails trimmed and buffed? Where did the fine but damaged dress come from?

She could have taken it. Isn't that why we are all here? Most of us, anyway. Guests of His Majesty for the crime of availing themselves of the property of others?

It would certainly be a feat to be enrobed in the very garment that had put her here.

No. This is her garment, her rich, but shabby fabric encasing her tall, spare person, her poor ankle not protected from the evil filth of this place.

"If you don't scratch it, I won't pick at my ear," I say, which I have begun to do.

She turns.

"Your ankle. We'll make it a game. You stop and I'll do the same."

She looks down at it then. I can see the red, raw skin on the inside of her ankle, peeking out beneath her skirt. I look back at her in time to see her eyes as well, just for a moment. Her face so fragile just then, I know she was born for better than this. Though I am smaller I know that she needs my hand, filthy though it is. I reach out and clasp hers and squeeze, and the tears spring forth and make clean trails down her pale cheeks.

"Oy! Wotcher playin' at? 'Appy Families?"

I round on them. I feel a rush through my being. It is only me. I am the same as always, but something in my swift turn, my sudden fire, silences them.

"Cur on the corner," I whisper to Caroline Lockett.

The worst of the winter is upon us. They say we'll be on the ship soon. March, they say. How long have we been here? The days are all one day, one long grey rag the dog drags behind him. You hold on because it I all you can do. But what day is it, today?

The guard says we'll be ready for the ship. He says that those of us going beyond the seas are damned. We will lose a lot more than our days.

I sit with Caroline Lockett when the food comes. We don't rush forward. We tilt our heads and look up at our prayers, trapped and twirling on the ceiling. I pray very hard and see a little burst of light just at the edge of my eye, one prayer escaping before the door is shut.

"Prisoners to prepare for departure," he is saying, *Prisoners to prepare.*

I look at Caroline Lockett. What do we have to ready for this event? She wore a rag of a tartan shawl for a time, but I see it now on another. Our shoes, our standing garments.

"I suppose we can't take the needlework frame," I whisper.

A twitch from Caroline Lockett.

"And we mustn't think of the vanity set."

A jerk of Caroline's head. I look up. A smile is playing on her face.

"You, girl, you just need cleaning up," the guard says to me.

Don't we all? I ignore his wicked stare as the women gather their bits and bobs.

"Can't imagine. Both of you. Can't imagine your journey. You'll sail to the colony on your backs, you will, like floatin', it'll be just like floatin,'" he cackles.

Caroline puts her hand on my arm but I turn to his pocked face, his dripping nose. "And you'll still be here, in this freezing hell, stepping in slop and sloughing off the dead, for the rest of your days." My mother. Mother always said it was my mouth. *Maura Quell, learn when it must stay shut.*

It must stay shut when the lips are swollen like this.

Caroline shakes her head. She somehow manages to get water from those who guard it, and I take the cup from her. The metal water is cool against my lips.

The curious ones are swarming. It happened in a trice.

It is when they start moving us out that they realize that Mildred Creek is dead.

I have no belongings, officially and unofficially. No jewelry. No shawl. No cloak. What I wear is in tatters, and my shoes may not hold out. I will be easy to move.

One girl, alone. No relatives. No belongings.

Maura Quell, you take care of the boy. You stay together.

Will the bitter tears never stop? Raining down the back streets, the steaming, reeking corners, the birds on posts, the old men curled up like buds.

London. I shall not miss you.

But Epping? The green. The forest, almost a being.

England? Nursery rhymes. Songs and airs in a pure voice unsullied by the day. Mother's hand on my forehead. Eugene's light breath caught in his nose, his small hiccough as he beetles behind me. Small legs and a big, big town, London town.

They think I weep for these lips that are swollen and bloody. They think I would actually cry for that.

The brilliant sun sets eyes on fire. Steeples glow and then fade out. Rubbing the eyes only adds gems and stars. It is a thing so beautiful and fleeting. It is so tragic. Lungs fill with air that has travelled the streets and factories, picked up stench and vapour from the tanners, the confectioner's sugar, the straw-hat maker's leavings, yes, even straw is in the air that wafts like water against the lighter. I have left the land.

The small boat plies the river.

O, Thames.

Is it sun? Or is it the eyes forcing it to be so after so long inside? Rain, sun, simple things that can be picked over and laid aside by choice. Caroline looks asleep, but perhaps she is merely breathing. They are all breathing, thinking. Much in distress. Has it become that much of a silent game? Even Hettie Rags Crenshaw is stifled as the ship looms in the near distance.

The groan of the oars. The groan of Molly whatsit, stole the feather bolster. None, now, to keep her warm.

The ship is called the *Canada*. We sail March 3 if all goes to plan. What day is today?

"My husband sailed on the *Spike* two years back."

"Aye, and have you heard of him since?" a voice asks.

"A letter. Nowt else."

Silence. The ship grows, mast and rigging. Ropes. Planks. Noises grow as well; now we can hear shouting.

We are seeds abob in the river. We are making for the sea.

If there were a way to walk upon the water, Maura, would you step out and walk back to shore?

Mother, I don't....

No, no, but if there were a way...but if. Yes, always that word for us, Maura, dear. If.

Mother.... If Eugene were on the shore, picking among the weeds; if Eugene looked up and saw the ship moored and the lighter making its way across to it; if Eugene shaded his blue eyes with his wee dirty hand.

Yes, Mother, yes. I would walk across the water to the shore.

It is called the *Canada*. Word is it is a former ship of war, taking a Spanish ship and engaging in battles years back.

"Battle of St. Kitt's, luv," says the boatman. "And now it's here to take you all into long ago."

Our chains keep us stumbling. We cannot stand properly. Even underfoot, the world changes. Even here, at anchor, there is a movement of the solid, a wavering. To stand is to sway, as though ingin-drenched stupor. And the prisoners, the itchy, abandoned females, glance down, uncertain of their feet.

One by one our fetters are hammered off with a clang.

"There go me clinkers," says Hettie Rags Crenshaw. She is weaving over to stand with the one they call Powder.

They line us up. The Ship's Surgeon, Matthews, will see us. The agent has passed papers across.

Eyes all round. Men in the rigging.

Where is Caroline Lockett? A shuffle of feet, a head craning. And there she is.

"Quitcher movin' about," a voice bellows.

I lift my hand to my crusted lip. It is but one quick tap.

"Ah…," the blood comes freely.

I move to the side to dab at my face, my sleeve smeared. But I move back far enough to find myself beside Caroline Lockett.

She edges back and I fall into line with her. I offer her one glance, as brief as a twitch, and I see her tiny nod.

"Next."

They ask questions but do not really wait for answers. To be truthful, many have no answers to give. The woman ahead petitioned to have her children brought aboard and was refused. She cannot speak for wailing. There was the one who lifted her skirts to reveal a horrible condition and was taken away immediately.

"Next."

"Quell, Maura."

Female, yes. Convict, yes. Age…thirteen. Health, generally good, yes, but for the ear, which nobody is concerned about.

Insolent? This has been listed beside other names. He does not know I can read. No reason to inform him.

He marks down my general condition. He notes my bleeding lip.

"How'd you get that?"

My hand goes up to the mess of my face.

"Fell. Fell, sir."

"You'd best be more careful. Ship's not a sturdy place."

"Sir."

He marks down "filth" beside my name.

O, Mother, would you not be giving him a piece of your mind?

To be huddled with the others is proof of desolation. Tears and blubbering from the lot of them. A few, like Hettie and Powder, are staking their claims early. Nothing will change here. Caroline Lockett is being shouted at. I push back to the line.

"Speak, before you are forced to!"

Her eyes are downcast but her face is resolute. She is jostled from behind, as if this will somehow loosen her tongue.

"She…she's dumb, sir. She cannot speak," I say, barely able to find the words myself.

The surgeon eyes me, then writes beside Caroline's name: "mute." I am shocked when he writes "incorrigible" as well.

Then he, too, becomes mute, pointing her to the side. I tap her shoulder and we go, like that, one with no voice and one with no proper lips to speak. She takes my hand and squeezes.

We are grouped together with four others and there is a grey-haired woman—Corn? Cord?—who will answer for us with the agent and procure our rations.

It is an old and serviceable vessel, they say. The deck is clean. There is an odour from somewhere that is terrible, but perhaps it is on the wind. The senior officer is barking instructions to the men, who fly this way and that. Some are midshipmen. Some are mates, who climb barefoot up the ropes.

It is wise to keep one's ears open, even as one holds one's mouth shut. There is much to learn. Everywhere are men mending, winding rope, tying, scrubbing. One mate scuttles over the side and disappears. He has been staring at Caroline for some time, so I am glad of his departure.

The woman whose children are lost to her has at last collapsed onto a coil of rope. None approach to comfort her. It is to be expected, as she was also denied her request while still in prison. She has relied upon mercy. She's a pitiable object, her face awash and completely wrung out.

It is cold on deck, but word is it is better than being down below.

"No air down there," is the whisper.

Always, the open window, small beetles on the sill, flowers in the broken cup. Mother standing there, her face framed, as Maura Quell, wanderer, returns home, her arms filled with faggots for the hearth.

O, Mother. I cannot be afraid.

Mother, I cannot show it. It is a game I play with the Law of England, the Newgate guards, and now the shipmates. And with Master Ward, who is transporting us away.

Away.

Cord...gives me the word and I look up. The midshipman's eyes are upon me, most inappropriately. Cord is nudging me. She is our voice on the ship yet she confounds me with her touch. What is it she wants?

"He's more than passing interested, if you have a mind."

Her voice not like Hettie's. She seems to regard the possibility with distaste that matches my own. I turn toward her and she frowns and puts an arm round me. Then I am alone.

There is a daily bread allowance. There is barley in the hold from which they'll make something they call burgoo or somesuch. I hear them talking. The meat is foul, what there is of it. They ask at the abattoir for the tough cuts of old and diseased meat. They can disguise it in the smiggins, but it is what it is. Like some of the women on this journey.

I watch the mates climb. This is something I would watch in the square, with coloured banners, with music and cheering. The mates listen to the pipe from somewhere; they follow commands I do not hear. Perhaps that is it. Perhaps we are all following commands we do not hear. I look over at Caroline Lockett who, if it is at all possible, has become even quieter since we boarded.

Incorrigible.

"Oy, we be ladies for a day, out on the Thames."

A cackle.

And then a lone voice crying. "I can't...please. I can't go down there. God help me, I can't...."

Desperate scuffling.

The stench from below is making some sick. There is no change of clothes for that one, so she begins the journey like that. I press my stomach closed with my thoughts. I force it to steady itself.

You are a stubborn girl, you are, Maura Quell.

33

Yes, Mother.

Your hem is gone in the back, Maura.

I look at my skirt, and I'm smiling when the midshipman catches my eye.

They are laying down the law. Cord will answer for us, and they want us to go to her with our problems and questions.

I'll sleep with one eye open.

Cord, the food, the air…. Cord is master of the very stuff of life. Doler of the lifelong gifts, like the gods of old, giving one the gift of foresight, and one miraculous strength.

Let's just assume life has not been easy for Aris. After all, look at her—twenty-first century woman, a professional—and yet Dr. Grogan feels she is on the edge of nothingness.

She wants to tell him he's wrong, to test the theory of nothingness having an edge, but when it comes down to it, she just doesn't have the energy. She stares at her toes as they block the TV screen. David Letterman is a foot with a cockscomb. When was the last time anyone touched her? The party at the art gallery? Her Christmas membership perk, and she'd been there drinking G&Ts and she smelled the Christmas trees in her glass, in the large main hall of the gallery. She bit into a lime slice. Just then, she was happy.

It must have rubbed off because she ended up in a taxi with an overdressed young gallery employee. Collections? Reference library? That was the last time.

David Letterman is talking her foot off.

Maura Quell. She wouldn't put it past her grandmother to make her up—a child bogeyman…a bogeychild?—to keep Aris in line. But the name stayed with her all these years, perhaps because it was so odd.

Not like hers, right, Aris?

She'd always hated her name. One whole year in school she was called Avis, thanks to a typo on the class list. Her other akas included Asshole Sandall, Sandy Ass and Candy Ass.

The fellow at the archives, who must also have had an interesting childhood (what was the name...Dunstan Regimbald?) promised her she would have things to work on, on her next visit.

Maura Quell.

She remembered her grandmother's voice. "Make your bed, Aris. Come along. You don't want to end up like that girl, Maura Quell."

She is reading the morning paper and is surprised to see a retrospective article about the girl in Alberta who was hooked up to a Berlin Heart, only to have her own heart repair itself as the girl awaited a transplant.

The Berlin Heart was enough on its own. This development—the article had called it a miracle—would take rethinking. And for some people, rewriting.

The Berlin Heart will allow a patient's own useless, damaged heart to rest so it heals itself. When removed, the Berlin Heart will also make muffins and will sponge-clean the furniture.

She looks at the photo of the young woman, holding in her hands her own personal miracle.

That's what she wants.

Not the Berlin Heart. The other part.

Monstrously stupid people live in her city.

Doorblocker:	So, did you get out of trig?
Pierced:	Fuck, no, man. They said it's too late to switch.
Doorblocker:	No way! Tell them you didn't know.
Pierced:	I did. They said too bad, so sad.
Doorblocker:	Brutal. So, did you study for the test?
Pierced:	No.

They crowd the door, like they're bouncers at an exclusive club, nodding this one in, waving that one away. A woman was trying to get off and they had to be cajoled and repeatedly tapped before they budged, and even then they only moved sideways so the woman had to battle her way out. A working woman, like herself, who looked like she was having a hard day. She had a few choice words for them.

    Doorblocker: D'ja hear her? Old bitch.
    Old bitch. Aris hangs on to the strap and sways inside the bus.

    Dunstan Regimbald is not in. It is his day off. Aris realizes that she hasn't mentally pencilled in a day off for Dunstan Regimbald. He works the service desk so, somehow, she has determined that he will always be there, his tie a bit askew, his hair a strange silhouette behind him.
    He has left a note for her with instructions. He has leapt at her speculation of 'prisoner' and taken it upon himself to assume that Maura Quell was brought to trial at some point. He has determined 'England' as Aris's grandmother had been English and it was her family tale. But when? Working backwards from Maura to her grandmother, the storyteller, and further back, he has given her a generous time range in which to search.
    So, England. A prisoner in England. Within the range of 1750-1875.
    "What? He wants me to look through a hundred and twenty-five years worth of documents?" Aris almost shouts.
    Today's reference desk librarian looks over.
    "That doesn't sound right," she says. "Here, let me see that. What is your relative's time frame? Birth and death dates?"
    Here we go again.
    "I don't know."
    The librarian hands the note back to Aris.

    Aris tries to get comfortable at the terminal. The green world undulates outside the window. She looks back at Dunstan's pinched handwriting.
    Old Bailey Sessions.

Might as well go for broke. And why not start there?

Dunstan Regimbald has printed, in what looks like fountain pen ink:

PATIENCE IS A VIRTUE. STUBBORNNESS KICKS ASS.

This is a bit odd, one might say unprofessional. Aris can't see today's desk clerk doing something like this. Dr. Grogan would say Mr. Regimbald is attempting to inject a little humour and spontaneity into the proceedings.

Dunston has also wished her: GOOD LUCK.

The Old Bailey Sessions.

The Old Bailey, to anyone who watches PBS, is a standby on British television drama, several highly competent English actors having graced the courtroom to plead, appeal, confess and condemn. It's on evenings like that, with a tea and biscuits, that Aris dreams about the trips not taken, the boyfriend who wanted her to travel with him to Istanbul, or at least, to New York.

The home page comes up.

Can this all be here, so neatly arranged, so organized? Who was drawn and quartered? Who was burned, who, dissected? Makes what Aris writes seem, all of a sudden, completely insignificant.

Your stent will require....

Her left cheek was burned with....

The trees wave in the picture windows. The tables glow. Aris sits at the cubicle desk.

I am a pawnbroker. I live in Shadwell.

I keep the Horn tavern by St. Paul's....

Are you sure you did not drop the watch out of your fob?

Aris thinks of the part-time uncles who came for turkey and punch, brothers of parents who got older each year as they performed their Christmas ritual. They were hardly real to her. They were her own blood and yet were hardly real.

Maura Quell.

A name? An inside joke the adults served up? Maura Quell, a girl. They always said a girl, not a woman.

I saw the back door open on the third Thursday in February....

Who are these people? They sound as interested in their whereabouts as she is in hers, and they are preoccupied with their details, the minutae of their lives.

I am sure he took it because I had it when I went out to the street.

Oh, your things. Your precious things. Your flat-screen TV, your personal GPS system. Your Berlin Heart.

My father lives in Soho. He's a brandy merchant. He is possessed...or was possessed of antique pewter....

What is it, Aris? What is so surprising about the fact that they are so possessive, so vain, so screwed?

She has missed her planned lunch break. She has skimmed over tens, maybe hundreds of names, crimes, punishments. She has not narrowed the search; she has not put Maura Quell's name to anything. She has come close.

Crime Category
Specific Criminal Act
General Verdict
Specific Verdict/Punishment
Crime Date
Victim Surname
Victim Gender
Defendant Surname
Defendant Gender
Defendant Age

There is where the name should go. It is all there is.

Something about these other voices, yelling, railing, pleading, something about them has her hesitating, sitting there while people whisper, while the photocopier hums and the coins drop and the weather turns outside and the storm comes up.

I am an officer....
I keep a lodging house....
I am. I keep.
I am. I keep.

Dark. And the stench. Which is worse, I don't rightly know. I am with Caroline. Cord has muscled us a space. It is terrible down here. I am dismayed to see that Cassie Jukes is among our lot. Her mouth is foul and she is repulsive. Caroline seems to know this because she puts herself between us.

Up above us, they climb the ropes, unfurl the sails. I do not know what else this ship carries. I have heard that the stores include victuals, fodder, material, plates, reels of twine, wine, biscuits. But for us, there is nowt, says Cord. And we have to divide that up.

The bilge is already reeking and we have not begun. There is all sorts down there, they say. Dead animals, peels, fabric, feces and all manner of waste. Even thinking of it brings me to my knees. How does the crew stand it, for they live with it as well?

The journey has begun. The ship moves. The motion is strange. Not a soothing motion, as mother used to do, when she rocked Eugene in the cradle. Or, if it is, then it is a monstrously big hand that bats at this cradle, rattling the timbers and making us walk as if on ice. How can we not know where the floor will be when it is below our feet? Because *below* changes and we must learn the new dance.

A hole. That's what they're all pushing to get to, a bit of light through a scuttle hole. Hettie Rags Crenshaw is plastering herself across it.

"O…London…," she says.

"Let me see, O, let me see once more!"

They cram and jostle.

Caroline crouches with me. Does she want one last look? One more stab to her poor heart? Can I look one more time on the shore, up the trailing ends of streets, one more time, to seek his fair, tiny head?

We crouch like two filthy statues, like guards at the gates of Hades.

Clearing the Thames Channel and heading out for open sea. We're locked down here until such time as they'll let us up on deck. I don't care if they make me scrub planks or clean slop. I could do so under the sun and the stars. In the open air.

I would empty my stomach in an instant if I didn't know I would have nowhere to clean myself. So I hold myself tight, put my body beside that of Caroline as the groaning and sloshing goes on.

I hear them, later, curled up in their tatters.

"I think I saw me mum on the shore."

"O, no, 'twas just those as come to watch."

"I saw the rooming house where I robbed old Mr. Duffy."

"My boy was there. My man had him in arms. I want my boy…."

Soon there will be no land around us at all. None. No thing to keep us rooted to the earth.

Sky. Water. We see neither. We feel the tread, we move and groan with the ship, we hear all manner of things. Clanging of the bell. O, Lord. Why is there always the bell? I think of the Executioner's Bell, then, and remind myself that this is the best possible outcome.

I feel unborn. Inside. As if I have yet to emerge into the world. And I could be anything yet, I could be a person of privilege, of talent, of youth and promise.

Caroline, my twin, waits beside me for the moment when we will be born together. New hope for the world, we are, to counter the viciousness, to foster the bright things just peeking out of the ground.

Caroline is scratching again. Would that there was a powder for it. Her ankle will bleed again and, then what, down here? I am afraid for her. I reach for her hand. Just my own on hers as she rubs. My hand's pressure, gently lifting, lifting her hand in mine. There. Now. Now.

"H-hurts…."

I am on fire. I shudder.

"Caroline!" I whisper, grasping her shoulders.

"Caroline!"

Calling her up from somewhere, from deep in Epping Forest, hiding from me, *Caroline*, it is my turn to hunt, to seek out and it is hers to hide.

"Caroline."

A creaky sound in her throat. A grunt from somewhere further in her chest.

"You speak?"

Neglected, rusted clockwork. Dusty and in need of someone's care. The slow whirring.

"…Maura."

Holding her face in my hands, in the dark with but a guttering lantern from somewhere. I see the gleam in her eyes. I feel like there is a bird between my hands. I feel I must close myself around her head, her ragged throat, her breaths in and out.

We say nothing. It is strange, but we say nothing at all. Words well up behind my eyes, but I hold her close, my friend. My friend Caroline.

We hear them opening up the barrel hatches. A mate scurries down the ladder. He calls us foul vermin. He has a tattoo on his arm, of a man carrying an anchor. I have seen many of the anchor, but this one is like an etching in one of the shops. He is telling us we must go up on deck. So they are piling toward the ladder. Up from the orlop to the 'tween-decks, he says, and then out through the hatch.

"Take it easy, watcher step, ladies," he cries, as one tumbles back onto those behind her. "Get yer rhythm out of it," he says. He knows. The sway is this way and that. You have to know the dance, like he does.

They proceed. We are at the back. I know, somehow, that I am not to tell Cord or anyone else about Caroline's voice. I am not to let them in on the secret.

The mate has his eyes on Caroline.

"You," I say through my scabbed lips. "Your tattoo. It's a fine one. What does it mean?"

"I means," he says, with one hand on the back of my dress, "It means I carries me 'opes with me."

I watch Caroline's crumpled shoes above me. I carry my hopes with me.

The sudden air and light are dizzying.

Is this what it is like to dance in the arms of a suitor? I sway, knees unsure. O, Maura, you shall fall, fall into his arms. My innards quake and my head swims. The world rises and falls beyond the rail.

Caroline is steadfast. They are showing us the heads, where we are to relieve ourselves while not in the hold. Terrible. There for all to view, under the sky, with not a cloth nor a sheet nor a shred of privacy.

They say we are to…to climb out from the bow-sprint, onto this plank with holes…. I cannot imagine. I cannot.

"Then…ye's washes up wit bucket," the mate explains. I look round. Who these women were, I know not, but never in their lives were they as low as they are now.

That is the case, then. By night we use the easing chairs, but by day—day, where we are visible to prisoners and crew alike—we are to tread to this primitive outpost and….

I hear a quiet chorus of "Never!" I hear the mates laughing. They know what we do not, and this fills me with a dread I have been prizing from myself.

"So, go on!" they laugh.

All of us. Suspended.

And then I see her. Feel her as she pushes away from my side, her dress grazing my arm. I see her press past Cord and Cassie Jukes. She says nothing, of course, for she is still wordless here. Everyone, including the agent and his mates, are caught by this sight, this slender woman who boosts up on a coil of rope, who swings out and makes her way along the platform. She reaches up behind her—how is she balancing like this?—and arranges her garment and then sits with her dress around her, a roosting hen, her feathers settling. We are caught by this. No one breathes or speaks.

Moments pass. She makes her way back along the plank. The bucket is there. I see her cup water in her hand, turn away from the witnesses, lose herself in her garments. Then she turns back. She looks up only once to face the stares, and it is a look such as I have not seen on this ship. I am beside myself.

There is a whoop from one of the men, and then a cheer, totally unwarranted. A woman I do not know the name of claps Caroline on the back as she makes her way over to me.

"And that," says the midshipman, "is how it is done."

It is the man who has had his eye on Caroline.

I'm told it's their right to take a partner for the voyage. They can choose someone; and it has already begun. The one they call Nessie has gone to the bed of midshipman Steeves. Bochum is after Ruby Wickes. And this one, named Harkness, I believe, this one wants Caroline.

Cord explains.

It is more than a custom, and in a way is a good thing. Cord says Caroline would be a fool to refuse. Better food. Better bed. Someone to protect her on board.

"But she's a girl," I speak for Caroline.

Cord reminds me that these are the ones that are chosen.

"They don't want the likes of me, do they?"

I know that Cord feels as I do, although whether for the self-preservation of young girls, or for her own desire to be chosen, I know not. I know, also, that Caroline does not wish it. We mean to keep her with us, though it is likely to be more difficult, now, with her public display on deck.

O, Maura, what is it you're thinking?

I know, Mother. She did it for us. But I am of two minds about it. She stepped up, but in doing so stepped away, separated herself from the rest of us and now I wonder whether she will do so with midshipman Harkness. It is only when I voice this to myself that I realize

I have come to expect her here, by my side. And now that I know she speaks I am desperate for a chance to whisper to her. And to have her whisper back.

❦

Aris has no pacemaker and yet her heart trips as the name search returns its findings:

Maura Quell
4 February 1809
Charge: Robbery
Verdict: Guilty
Punishment: Transportation

Aris rises from her seat before the terminal. She looks left and right. A man with headphones on, typing. A woman with a cart at the end of the reading room.
She wants to shriek.
She remembers her grandmother's felt hat, the one with the pearl hatpin. How Aris watched the pin disappear into her grandmother's head, the drone of the voice unchanging.
She remembers the balled-up handkerchief in the old woman's sleeve, and the several in her cardigan pocket. Her hard Taverner's fruit drops dusty in the tin beside her.
Aris, you haven't finished your cauliflower. Mind you do. You don't want to end up like that girl, Maura Quell.
That girl. All of thirteen. That Maura Quell.

She needs a tea to settle her nerves. She is exhibiting all of the symptoms of an angina attack.

Your current medication notwithstanding, it might be prudent to consider bypass surgery.
Or perhaps an artificial heart. Or two.

The cafeteria is patronized by staff who can't leave the building for any place better in an hour, and by researchers like her.

A researcher. Not a lawn-bowler, Dr. Grogan.

A genealogical researcher.

She's too excited to eat the salad she'd fluffed onto her plate. She's overdone it with the dressing, nullifying the salad's positive impact. She's eating neutral, and what's the point of that?

Her Earl Grey is steeping. She thinks back to the name on the strangely glowing screen.

Doesn't mean she's a relative, she's quick to remind herself. Could be a name out of a hat. Or somebody the family read about once. Like saying you're related to the Queen of England. Or cousin of Prince Charles, like Vera used to say on *Coronation Street.*

But it does say one thing.

Someone named Maura Quell existed.

"Hello."

She looks up. The tucked-in waist of the reference librarian, Dunstan Regimbald.

"Do you mind?" He gestures to the seat opposite her.

"Uh...no...no, go ahead. Only I'm almost done."

Probably what he was hoping she'd say. He has some kind of fish filet on his plate, smothered in a cream sauce. He's eating neutral as well.

"So," he says, "any luck?"

This is when Aris realizes she has been waiting for him to show up. He is precisely the person she wants to tell.

"I found her. Her crime. I found a name with a crime."

"Good. Very good. You have a time frame now."

It is nothing more than that? Can't he see it is so much more than that?

"You don't underst...my family never said if she...whether she was real. All this time. I was never certain, you know? I mean, I almost passed out when I saw her name."

Dunstan nodded, using his knife to probe the fish.

"I see it all the time. Wonder. Delight."

He reaches for his roll.

"You see it all the time? Well, lucky you."

He looks up.

"I know."

He wants her to tell him how far she has followed the trail.

"What? I just found this. I don't know what comes next."

He smiles. "And isn't it exciting?"

Aris finds herself picking at her salad just so she can talk to this man. He is supremely ordinary, eating his meal indifferently, adjusting his glasses, getting up to procure extra tartar sauce.

Your current eating habits almost certainly guarantee a return visit to hospital, when you may be asked to take part in our survey and our voluntary monitoring project.

She ponders what he has told her. He is certainly the first person she's bumped into lately who says he sees wonder all the time.

If she will wait for him, he'll head up to the Reading Room with her to look over her findings. Aris sits and, for a moment, a little of that wonder seeps onto her plate.

Dunstan Regimbald asks if she is ready. Aris nods.

"There. Transcript of the trial. Or would you like to read it in the original?"

"The original?"

"The actual transcripts, not the current spellings and fonts."

"Uh...okay."

He clicks on "Original" and the document appears.

"Double felony...she...."

Dunstan whisks the air with his hand. "She's like most of them. Got caught stealing clothing, or material. See?"

48

"A...she took a shirt? She took a goddamn shirt?"

The Reading Room responds to Aris's enthusiasm with a collective glare. The man going by with the cart of books pauses.

"What...," she sees Dunstan's hand gesture for silence, "what," she whispers raggedly, "does it mean?"

"Read on," he opens his hand to the screen.

"Capital...capital offence? She took a shirt!"

"Tough times," Dunstan Regimbald replies.

Aris reads silently, her lips moving, recreating the changes. "Seven years? What is this...transport beyond the seas? What's that?"

"That," says Dunstan, "is the euphemism for convict ships to New South Wales."

A chill creeps into her mid-back area. Australia?

"Maura Quell was sent to Australia?"

Dunstan is clicking back to an earlier point. "It would appear that she was. See? I'd noticed it on the summary, here, but I didn't want you getting ahead of yourself."

Australia. The child, only found now in England, has already moved in Aris's mind.

"Well, what about her family? What would her parents have said or done?"

The reference librarian pauses. "No mention of them in the trial proceedings. I would expect she was an orphan. No address, no home base, if you will. No one to miss you if you left. I expect she was probably alone."

Aris feels a queasiness, a hatpin stab in the heart.

Undoubtedly, you will have to get used to the functioning of your heart in the post-infarction period.

Aris is not a mother. She has never had the so-called joy of reproducing. She has held very few children in her
life. But something hurts wickedly at the thought of this child on the streets. Stealing. Her capture. Her trial. Alone.

"Can you say that for sure?"

49

Aris's head is swimming. Her arm aches. Maybe she is having a heart attack.

"I don't...feel well."

"You're really feeling poorly?" He places a hand on her arm.

What is this? Concern from the rumpled man?

She just wants to close her eyes a moment, but he is getting her up from her chair and taking her into a staff lounge down the hall. The fluorescent lights make it worse, but she doesn't want to say, so she sits, slumped, on the leather sofa.

"Sometimes it's a shock," he says, as he puts the kettle on.

She can't stand the way he makes this sound. Like it happens every day. He hasn't got a clue what she's going through.

"They...others...they think they're looking for names and dates, and then they meet people."

It's just that this girl has suddenly stepped out of Aris's childhood stories and into a time and place, like God has just stuck her on Cherry Street, or Cowl Lane, in 1809 or 1952. It is so random.

"The others," he continues. "They can't believe that the people lived...I mean, *lived*. It takes a little getting used to. Do you go to cemeteries?"

What is this man babbling about? He's a cheerleading Druid.

"Here. Tea. Tea solves everything."

Aris manages a bit of a smile.

"Now you sound like my grandmother."

"The one who used to tell you about your subject, here?"

"That's just it, she never did. If she had told me, I wouldn't be here today."

"Enjoying the Celestial Seasonings tea," he adds.

"Yes." This smile is for real.

She wants to know what comes next. But, at the same time, she wants to be careful. There is a lot to take in and she doesn't want one huge information drop and then nothing. That was the way it always feels at work. She doesn't hear from the boss for a week and then—bam—information drop. Files, projects, overdue need-

'em-now documents. It always reminds her of the propaganda drops she read about that happened during the war. The planes would drop tons of pamphlets over the cities; it would snow pamphlets.

She doesn't want that here. Not for the girl. Not for Maura Quell.

"Go home. Sleep. Come back."

Does he read minds?

"Hey, I do go to work as well, you know," Aris says.

"Of course." Adjusts his glasses. "I mean, next time you come maybe you can look at prison records."

"Do you spend this much time with all your library clients?"

Why has she said that? She's ruined it now. Does she think he's trying to come on to her?

"Certain clients require more guidance," he says, holding the door for her. As she steps through he adds, "But very few get my private stash of tea."

God, he's being genteel.

The wind has died down but a light rain falls as she stands in the bus shelter. There is a large advertisement for a charitable foundation's lottery. She could win big.

The bus turns the corner and as it approaches Aris notices a girl running for the stop. Her knapsack bounces on her back, her ponytail bobs. Twelve. Thirteen. Aris stands with one foot on the bus step and waits.

Her grandmother could play piano by ear. She could hear a song once and it would be hers. When her grandmother sat at the bench, back a little bent despite her self-admonitions, she looked small, and Aris could almost imagine her as a child, before life had her burying her own children.

She would sit and, Aris supposed, call up a song from some time in the past, and she would put her stiff fingers to the keys. Silly songs from the old days in England. "Everything is tickety-boo," she'd sing, her voice strong despite her size.

She played old dirges, she called them, stopping to pop a Taverner's fruit drop into her mouth. These were mostly wordless, meandering ventures up briar paths, down country lanes, and into the arms of pale lads long since dust.

Aris would sit looking at the woman's face and wondering who she was.

Now, mind you don't kick at the piano.

The upright piano with the scuff marks from Aris's Hush Puppies.

Aris sits with her Earl Grey. Maybe Dunstan Regimbald is right. Maybe it is always better with tea.

A hard and restless night, the ship rolling, creaking. In my sleep Caroline Lockett came, lifted a scabbed hand to my face and pushed back my hair. Then she leaned in and began whispering to me. Her voice, it was so low at first that I very nearly missed it for the rush of wind in the trees. We were in Epping. Caroline's dress was fine, the fabric whole and unsoiled. Her cheeks were not sallow, her hair clean and shining. Only the hands were the same.

And the voice? She leaned in and I could feel her breath on my shoulder. And then it came forth and was a lad's voice, gruff and insistent, a young man warning me of something, some thing. And I listened but could not understand the meaning of the words.

When I awoke I saw her back up against the beam, asleep on her feet. Cord has been watching, though she swears she is not looking out for her. Midshipman Harkness has been prowling. He is fit and upstanding enough, compared with many on this ship. And, truth to tell, many of the men are already matched. Cord is too old. Cassie Jukes, too repulsive. But many of the women are passable to these men, the younger the better, as they say. And more will be passable as the journey continues.

I have reason to believe I am also being sought. This is nothing definite but I feel eyes on me when I walk on deck, and there is a young mate that turns his face from me whenever I look up to the rigging.

Caroline sleeps, dreams, perhaps. Is she holding up a mast for us now?

"You, girl, you come over here and warm me toes."

This is what comes from sitting up, awake, in the night.

Where are we? I should like to know. How far from…it was going to be "home" but there is no home for us at all now. How far are we from our destination then? I am a bead of dew on a leaf, sliding around aimlessly. A rabbit on a frozen pond, all directions leading to white.

My heart jumps when I think of us alone here, under God's sky. As if we are the whole world, here on the ship. If this is true, who, then, are the worthy among us? Who the kindly people? The priests? Who is the man I would marry? And where, on the ship, are my children?

Today, torrents rip across the desk. We cannot go up. The easing chairs are full, the air is foul. Sickness all over. Nobody speaking except to curse or pray. I have not had one moment with Caroline Lockett.

Has she purposefully pressed herself as far away from me as possible? The flame flickers in the lantern. Everyone flickers, their edges change in this light, they are made of wax, and beautiful.

Except those in the corner. Their voices rise, now, a cackle. Cassie Jukes holding forth. I try not to hear them. Not to hear her.

"Out of their pinnies in a trice. Ye can't believe how easy it were. 'Cepting when they'd wail, o' course. I do hate a brat that wails. Nowt to do but cuff 'em and stuff 'em, right?"

Her common horrors.

"'E's all about wanting to hold on to 'is pitiful shoes. Like he's a right to 'em."

What is she on about?

"'Magine it, little tub no biggern' oat bag, an 'e's fightin' me fer a pair of shoes wit' the soles all gone on 'em."

They are hiding in the forest. Maura tells him to make sure to hide all of himself, not to leave his telltale yellow sleeve showing. She tells him she will wait through an entire hymn before she comes looking.

As heaven's clouds open and she enters paradise, she stops singing, turns, and calls out to him, *Eugene! I'm coming to find you! Here I come!*

On those legs he cannot have gone very far. But she makes a game of it as she watches the green moving back and forth in the breeze.

He is there, of course, his yellow sleeve almost a late leaf, but his fair hair is no nest, no blossom. She looks the other way and calls. *Eugene! O, where have you got to? You do hide so well.*

Then she moves in on the tree. His little foot is right there. Right there.

"But, Cassie, whatcha do wit' them babies and kiddies?"
"Takes 'em by their tow-'eaded curls and…."
The ship heaves.
Eugene.
"Ah, look at you, lass. What a mess you are."
Cord finds a bucket with some water. She taking her own headscarf off and dipping it and wiping down my front.
Caroline Lockett's eyes watch from the corner.

✼

"You know, so much of this is available online now. You really don't have to come all the way in. Now that you're more comfortable with searching, you might want to try something like *ancestry.ca* and work from home."

Aris looks up from her notes.

"Are you trying to get rid of me?"

The reference librarian shakes her head.

"Not at all. This is a public service. We want citizens to use their resources."

"Okay, then," Aris bristles. The last thing she needs is something that will isolate her at home, which is why she doesn't have a PC or a laptop. After spending all day in the oatmeal enclosure, she longs for the wide open spaces of, say, the kitchen.

Re: Diabetes and so-called "Silent Heart Attacks"

The patient with multiple health concerns needs to be vigilant when it comes to maintaining a balance....

She is relived when Dunstan Regimbald comes back from his day off, and she's delighted to hear that he has passenger lists, and convict lists as well, for her to go through.

This...child. It's strange. Aris supposes she never truly believed in Maura Quell. She was like "Mistress Mary, Quite Contrary." "Little Boy Blue."

"Conditions in the prison," Dunstan Regimbald tells her, "were grim."

He has offered her texts which describe deplorable circumstances, people dying underfoot, 'gaol fever', vermin. And cold. Aris has always been particularly susceptible to cold, wrapping not one but two scarves, one inner, one outer, around her neck in winter.

It made so-called winter sports all but impossible, except for the single perfect days of sun and warmth. Aris would fling herself into the day with an intensity and an expectation that always ended up disappointing her. There's a lesson there, Aris.

"You know, old stone buildings like nunneries and prisons were terrible for things like rheumatism and arthritis. T.B., too."

Old peoples' diseases, surely. Not for someone like Maura.

"So, you think she's an orphan, then?"

Dunstan Regimbald shrugs. "It would seem so. Given her testimony. She states no living parents. And given her activity in the street. Here, look."

"I took but one thing, Sir."

A shirt. And here's the magistrate:

"And what did you do with it then?"

She talks about trying to sell it. She doesn't take it home."

"Doesn't mean...."

"She hasn't got a home to go to, see? And there's no family in court, no one to speak for her, or to cry out when she is sentenced. There were...there were a lot of children on their own on the streets of London back then."

"I've seen *Oliver*, thanks. Do they all break into song?"

Why is she getting angry with the man for stating the obvious? Does she honestly think that because the idea of a child alone in the world offends her sensibility it will make one bit of difference to anything? Listen to the lot of them.

I didn't get me wages, and he was all the time flogging me. So this day in question, M'Lud, I jest took what was mine.

He made off with me good name, Sir.

My baby was ill. It had croup and I was beside myself. It died, Your Honour, not long after.

I hit him. I'da hit him again but he went down on the first blow. I know I'll swing for it, but he had it coming.

What would you recommend for them, Dr. Grogan? Line-dancing?

"The other reason I think she was on her own is that she didn't belong to a church, a parish. In her judgment it clearly states 'without benefit of clergy.'"

"What's that?"

"Without benefit? The church could step in. Back in the Middle Ages people convicted of felonies might be turned over to their respective churches to be dealt with by them. At the time this girl was on trial she might still have been able to claim benefit of clergy because they didn't abolish it completely until 1820."

Dunstan Regimbald pauses to clean his glasses. Aris ponders this man who is possessed of such fiber-optic strands of information. His eyes are watery.

"I'm sorry," he says, and she feels him reading her mind. "I get a little carried away. I...really am interested in this sort of thing."

"I can see that."

Aris doesn't understand these elderly young people. Here's her doctor telling her to get out into life, and then here is this man holed up with the velvet hum of the photocopy machine.

"So you are saying it's unlikely she had family because she wasn't in a church?"

"Signs. They're all signs. She had no adult to speak for her, no character witness. She had no excuse when she was caught. It's not like she was bringing the merchandise home to mother."

"I see," Aris said.

"Transport wasn't the worst that could have happened to her. Even with benefit of clergy, up until 1779 she would have been branded....I...I'm doing it again, aren't I?"

When Aris was seven, a boy in her class was caught stealing from another child. The teacher marched the boy outside at recess, where he stood on a chair, wearing a paper dunce cap that had THIEF written on it in chalk. Most of the children could not read the word but had a glorious time bumping the chair, trying to knock the boy off his perch, and pelting him with clods of earth dug up at the school fence.

What had Maura Quell seen and heard?

"You really might want to acquaint yourself with the prison conditions while you're searching. She would surely have spent some time in Newgate."

"You're sure she'd be in Newgate?"

"Yes. The Old Bailey was the 'court of gaol delivery' for Newgate."

Enter Rumpole and Kavanagh, Q.C..

"So, who would have turned her in? This Mr. Butler, the shopkeeper?"

"General hue and cry, I should think."

"Sorry?"

"You know. Butler himself, or anyone in the shop. A constable or a city marshall would have picked her up."

"She must have been so scared."

"I would think," Dunstan says as he is called back to the desk.

Aris sits with the judgement back up on the screen. She has exercised the option of reading it in the original version, which is harder on the eyes but which somehow feels closer to the truth.

But what is the truth? Maura Quell. Who existed after all. What is it Dunstan has said—how in the old days they used to brand the thumb with a "T" if you were a thief? Before Maura's time, perhaps. Better than branding the cheek, which was also done. Yes, this Dunstan Regimbald and his strands like some kind of primitive jellyfish.

What would be worth stealing? Aris can't imagine. But then, Aris isn't hungry. Aris is sick to death of her lifestyle and her diet but that is not the same thing as being hungry. Twice when Aris was a child she'd been sent to bed without supper, but this was the extent of physical deprivation. She'd missed a high school dance. She was denied a school trip.

Later, sitting with a curry in the market restaurant, Aris can't decide what would be worse, rotting in a horrible prison or being sent halfway around the world.

At work, there is a statement due on the latest stent study. A response-piece, measured, taking all things into account. Don't sound dismissive. Give credit where it is due. Promote the product.

Aris knows two people who have stents—one is a cousin and the other is a neighbour on her street who dropped at the corner on her way to buy her lotto ticket. Mrs. Bradshaw was in hospital and a few days later came back with a new attitude and a stent in her chest. Aris's cousin Colleen, too, was benefitting from the device. So why does it feel like she's selling snake oil off the back of a cart?

Getcher super-adaptable, rapidly-disappearing Stentomatic here, folks. They're goin' fast, fast, fast. Better them 'n you, right? Right! Now, line up on the left.

The boss has been giving her the arched brow lately. He sees her carrying files home. Planning on billing for overtime? Selling off company secrets?

Aris opens her desk drawer, sees the dark navy file with "QUELL" on the label.

Screw you, she smiles at the boss as he makes a pass, like a shark, by her cubicle.

In the bunk with Caroline Lockett. There was a third, Maeve, or somesuch Irish, but she has been moved down. We are side by side, up against the hull, our heads almost touching the very ark. Perhaps sailors in passing ships will see the shape of our heads as we dream our way to Botany Bay.

I do not know why I fell so suddenly ill, only that I felt faint and sick all at once, and then Cord was sponging me off and Caroline was putting me to bed here. Fever? I do not know. I feel neither fevered nor chilled.

She is up close beside me; I smell her hair and her odour. And when she speaks into my ear I am sure I am the only one who hears her.

"Cassie Jukes," she is saying that hated name. "It was Cassie Jukes as was talking."

It was the dream.

"Eugene," I began. "It was our Eugene." She holds my hand in hers. I have only a little story of a little boy that is of no importance to the world. The birthmark on his neck, the blue of his eyes, no concern to the world. His loving gaze, the fineness of his cheek, nothing to anyone at all.

Caroline listens, and she whispers back.

"Your brother is with God?"

And forgive me, forgive me, but I have no comfort in that. I see only his tired face, his running nose and his broken down shoes. And I turn to Caroline Lockett, to her brave and honest face, and cannot tell her the next thing that is in my heart.

The weather is brisk and we are allowed up on deck. We are in blue water now, and this has eased the restrictions. There is work to do, scrubbing, washing, sewing. Harkness has taken it upon himself to present Caroline Lockett with a shell. A shell! If he had found, perhaps, a book of ancient poetry, a fan from a lady's chamber. But a shell. It is pretty enough. Caroline shows it to me as we walk the deck. She has been given a needle and some cotton shirts to mend. I sit and ask for the same.

A needle. How I searched for one when Eugene's clothes came apart. A needle and thread, such as mother had by the hearth, but none was to be found. Surely this is when one knows one is penniless. And now, with nothing in the future but this churning sea, a needle and thread. And a shell.

Harkness doesn't know that Caroline speaks. She believes she is as silent as the wind in a doldrums.

"Why don't you tell him?" I ask her. For in truth, I do not know why she keeps it a secret. Perhaps it saved her from harm as a witness back where she same from, but that can hardly matter now.

"Do you want him?" I ask, for I may as well know if I will be losing my bunk mate to him.

She shakes her head but she keeps the shell hidden behind the rags at the head of our berth.

The lad in the ropes looks down at us. He is young, though older than either of us. Sandy-haired beneath his cap, his tied hair protruding from the back. He answers to the name of Marsh. They go about their business, these mates, as we go about ours.

Caroline spreads the shirt open to examine the seam.

"Cassie Jukes," she mumbles as Herself arrives up on deck. She is actually chatting the heels off a midshipman who has no time for this nonsense. On to the next. Perhaps there was a time when she had enough glimmer and vinegar to capture the eye of a lonely man. Not now. She parades, pathetically, and I should like a mast to fall on her head.

"I think I shall kill her."

I say it before I think it. Caroline gawks, then grabs my arm, pulls me roughly and the needle pricks my skin.

"No" she spits as I cry out.

I put my finger to my lips and taste blood.

She doesn't know. She was not there when my dream told me all. I remember it now.

Cassie Jukes, her heaving breasts beneath the stolen shawl, her grotesque smile, holding out her hand to Eugene as he cries up from the cobbles.

"Here you are, here, are you lost? Well, come on, then. Come to Auntie Cassie. Eh? I'll see to you well enough. Watcher warbling on about, eh? Come on, boy."

Dangling her hand out like a rope off the side of a ship.

Caroline was not there to see Eugene pick himself up from the dust and grit and look at her with questioning eyes before proffering his own hand, his arm in the outgrown coat that is worth whatever can be got for it.

Everything is clear as we sit in the sun, Caroline Lockett scratching her ankle with the needle. She nods me to look aft, where Marsh is setting to holystone a piece of the deck. Someone, an Irish, sings a dirge that they are so good at. It rises and falls like this ship.

This is to be our fate for months. The Atlantic Ocean is full of secrets: gold coins, silver-plate from doomed vessels, the vessels themselves. But bones? Bones disappearing even as flesh does; bones would wash down, wouldn't they? Gone. Wretched bent fingers, rotting teeth, breath just bubbles on the underwater current.

Maura Quell, if you haven't got the worst ideas, girl. Come inside and sit by the hearth. What are you doing out there on the stoop?

They are playing cards. They gamble for everything, for bits of salt horse, a quaff of the daily drink, a moldy potato, a broken hair comb. They have made themselves a deck of cards from the pages of a Bible that poor Mathilda Hubbs had stashed in her bunk. There are a few who refuse to take part, due to the blasphemous nature of the proceedings, but most break down and play a hand, as most cannot read the pages anyway.

Crudely-drawn pictures and numbers grace the pages, and the hoots and hollers fly from the bunks down at the end. One poor fool has just lost her cloak. She will miss that when the winds start up again. They dropped a page at the end of their game, or perhaps it became attached to someone's foot, for it is terribly stained when I find it on the floor. I see that it is from the Book of Wisdom. And I read this:

For in secret
the holy children of good people offered sacrifices,
and with one accord agreed to the divine law,
so that the saints would share alike the same things,
but blessings and dangers....

    I thought about this even as one of Cassie's minions snatched the page from my hand.

    Capetown. A long way off. But it is on everyone's lips, a name, at least, a *town*.
    I feel as if I have been on board always, as if this is the only world, and all of the other places merely scribbled dreams. Epping, a green dream of forests and wondrous beasts. London, a city of coal-black boulders, black and garnet streets, wisps of gray cotton at the edges of laneways.
    A shirt of cambray, a waistcoat embroidered so finely with stitches that cannot be seen. Shops brimming with silk ascots, carved mahogany walking-sticks, gloves as soft as the breast of a linnet.
    Was it real? The smell of leather tanning. The gurgle of the water in the roadside gully-hole.

My love, my love. Your hair, it has gone gray
Your breath is faint and faltering,
And I have gone away....

    What was it? How did it go?

I am humming to myself as I braid an oily rope. As I am studying Cassie Jukes.

One, now two, have fallen ill. We are given an elixer; I do not know what it is, but that it has lime and vinegar, that I know. They worry for the scurvy, when they should worry for other things. The rats, the filth, bugs that bite and drain us in the night. Caroline Lockett has opened her ankle again. I have begged her to attend the surgeon over it. She shakes her head and is suddenly mute again, as if it is an affliction which comes and goes.

I wish to know how, why, it is she will not speak. She can read, this much I know, for I see her scanning such few things on board as have words attached. Her eye runs over the letter that Norris tucked aboard. We have all heard those goodbyes a hundred times.

An me own, me darlin Dotter,
I love ye and wil wait yer Returne

You will await Norris, for fourteen years, to my seven. Had she killed someone? It is said she seduced a gentleman and then ran him through with a poker, for his funds. She was caught with his mother of pearl-handled walking stick. So they say. She seems to all of us a mild sort, although there is that scar on her forearm.

We have been told that few if any ever return. For how would one pay for passage on a journey of this length? Seven years, for many, would be too long a time gone, never mind fourteen.

Look at them. Their bodies are already betraying them. The heavy, heavy air is weighing them down, hands pressing on shoulders, leadening the legs. The salt water stiffens their skin. Soon they will be statues, figureheads as grace the prows of ships, and what strange-looking figureheads, frozen with their eyes wide open, speechless but for the wisps of words clinging to their lips.

So it goes aboard the *Canada*, a ship named for a far-flung colony. The *Canada* sailing the wrong way on the ocean, no homing bird she, with an eye toward her own shore.

Maura, dear, be a love and stoke the fire. My back is gone today and I can't rise for the pain.

Yes, mother. You really should eat something. There's some porridge left. I can ladle you some.

Mother, too, in the heavy, heavy air. Land-bound but breathing in the weight of it all.

✤

Aris is thinking about what Dunstan said. How you could buy your way up in prison to a slightly better set of circumstances. Not a bed or anything, necessarily, but something more than a stone. This Maura was alone, though. There'd have been no relief for her.

Eye makeup:	Mr. Carlson threw me out in the middle of the test.
Pierced lip:	What? He can't do that. Why did he throw you out?
Eye:	The man is a fucking psycho. He gets all in your face for anything. He took my cell and wouldn't give it back 'til the end of the day.
Lip:	He...he took your cell?
Eye:	I couldn't text Matt 'til I got it after school.
Lip:	Maybe he thought you were cheating.
Eye:	Cheating? I don't care about his fucking exam. I'm failing anyway.

The bus picks up and drops off the populace. Some are regulars. Aris has noticed the earnest man in the front, who always sits by the driver and who always gives up his seat to someone. She has wondered why he doesn't choose another seat right from the start but has concluded that he is a seat saver. He keeps the seat for someone more worthy. Not as glamorous a job as those celebrity seat holders at the Academy Awards whose posteriors are employed in keeping seats full for the inevitable pan shot camera-swoop.

I sat in Marisa Tomei's seat.

I was Jim Carrey.

Well, his ass, anyway.

There is the woman who reads the tomes. What they are, nobody knows, for she covers the books with the same brown cloth cover. It is edged in gilt, which keeps it from looking like a plain brown wrapper. Aris knows that they are different books, week after week, because she has watched the bookmark move day by day.

Aviation repair manuals?

The Bible?

A steamy romance, bodice ripping beneath the plain cloth cover?

No expression on the woman's face. No difference whether they are calibrating altimeters or caressing breasts.

Aris is hit by a knapsack as the school world disembarks.

Look happier, she wants to tell them.

She can see Maura among them. She isn't too tall, as females aren't back then, and without proper nutrition.... She is a slight girl of medium height, around five feet or so. Her figure is slight which looks fine in tight jeans, but she isn't wearing them. Plain corduroy pants. A striped sweater. She can afford the horizontal stripes. Bright but not too bright greens, blues and a touch of rust. A long scarf wrapped round, schoolboy style. And a poor-boy hat. A green knapsack—no, brown. She fits right in, filing to the front doors to head toclass. She looks back as she reaches the entrance. Has she forgotten something? A glance over her shoulder. A smile.

"So, Aris, you're feeling better since our last visit?"

Dr. Grogan is pleased with his creation, Victor Frankenstein marvelling at what a bit of cat gut and ingenuity can achieve.

"You're looking well," he adds.

"I'm keeping busy, Work is busy."

"And the other? The hobby front?"

She might like him better if his words didn't conjure such absurd images, the battles of Vimy and Passchendale peppered with soldiers building card-houses and collecting spoons.

Dunstan Regimbald is waiting for her when she arrives. This is not true. He is at the Reference Desk and is actually busy enough without her attendance, but he perks up when she walks in. Has she seen him brighten at her entry?

"You can check the Ships Lists for this period, here," he says with perhaps more interest than he has just shown the previous client.

"Okay. What am I looking for, exactly?"

"Well…her. She'd have been sentenced, then returned to prison to await the next fleet."

"They sent them out in batches?"

"Well, sort of," he says. "They sent the First Fleet off in 1787. It took them forever, most of a year. The Second Fleet went out in 1790. Worst fleet by far. Be glad she wasn't on that one. It wasn't a large fleet but it was brutal…the conditions, the deaths on board. Third Fleet sailed 1791, and Transport got more regular after that. She'd have been awaiting the next available ship which, given her conviction date, would have been in 1810, I expect. So you can go through the Ship's Lists for that period."

The web-site comes up immediately. It is well-organized, with ships, ports, and sailing dates.

"Okay," she says, and settles into her familiar chair.

It is strange, the metamorphosis that has taken place. When Aris was a child, her grandmother spoke of Australia as if it was the end of the earth and the home of murderers. Strange now to see the care that has gone into this elaborate documentation.

She scrolls through sailing dates, ship names, the *Bengal Merchant*, the *Mangles*, the *Neptune*, the *Earl Grey*. And the names of convicts. It is the same sensation as going through the court documents. So many names, people hardly real to her until one stands out. One.

Maura Quell.

"I found her!"

Aris can't believe it. Is she crying? What a fool. "Look! Here. But why does it say '*Canada*?'"

"Ah…yes. She's sailing on the *Canada*. See? March 23, 1810, aboard the *Canada*. A converted warship, likely. At this period a lot of the older ships that had seen service in the Napoleonic War were converted to take on prisoners. And, see, there's a "2" after the name. That means it was on its second voyage as a convict ship. Good find."

She is absurdly happy to see the name on the screen.

"The ship sailed March 23, 1810 out of England. Ship's Master was John B. Ward. She sailed to New South Wales."

"Australia," he says.

"It took 169 days."

"Not too bad, actually. As I say, the First Fleet took about half again as long."

She realizes at once. "You already knew this. You've already looked it up."

Dunstan Regimbald feigns shock. "I didn't!" Then he adds, "I didn't but I could have. I saw the site and the lists. But I thought it would be better if you found it."

Aris doesn't know what to say. She feels both grateful and irritated that this man has this control over her…her joy.

He looks at her and is reading her mind again and says, "Didn't it…didn't it feel good to discover it?"

"Did I feel the wonder, you mean?"

It sounds nastier than she wants it to. He looks hurt. What is she doing? She knows she has said something wrong. She focuses back on the screen.

"So…she spent months in prison *after* her conviction, and then set sail. For Sydney?"

Out of the corner of her eye Aris can see him nodding.

"What's this? One hundred and twenty-two females aboard. No males?"

"No male convicts."

"And one hundred and twenty-one on arrival."

"One death," he murmurs.

Dunstan's glasses again. He cleans them methodically.

"A death on board?"

"Only one perished, yes. A fairly humane crossing, it would seem."

He is called away to the desk and seems relieved to go. Aris watches the trees outside the window, and the sickly yellow sun. One hundred and sixty-nine days at sea. All those nights falling asleep praying, crying or cursing. Alone.

This, you want to tell Dunstan Regimbald, this is getting into my heart.

There is a card posted by the mailboxes. Someone has kittens to give away. Does that mean they are already in the building? There has been a discussion about pets. Cats were raised. Dogs, of the small breeds, anyway. Responsibility she didn't need. But love? Dr. Grogan believed that love was achievable with the right house-trained animal, preferably some creature that was no longer able to breed, but that required walking and exercise.

Free To A Good Home

Meaning, of course, that they would charge a fee to a bad one.

She was rude to Dunstan Regimbald. She hadn't meant to be. She was so excited to see the name, to find Maura Quell again. That's what it felt like, like Maura was out there in the abyss and Aris had claimed her. And, somehow, the idea of Dunstan Regimbald hovering nearby, both literally and figuratively, bothered her. It cheapened the find somehow.

The fact that he has helped her find the girl—the fact that if he had not assisted her she wouldn't have known where to start—is not lost on Aris. She will have to offer to buy him a coffee or something, next time she is there.

The *Canada*. A foreboding ship? An old warship pressed into service, hoovering up the refuse from the English and Irish shores, plying the ocean waters for 169 days.

Aris turns on the TV. David Letterman. What has happened to his smug and smart-ass youth? He seems weary now, less sure of the world. They all are. Don't even get her started on Leno.

When she was a student and stayed up late studying or reading, she'd often put on late night TV and wait for the psychics. The post-2:00 a.m. airwaves were full of pizza parlours, vacuum

71

cleaners, and psychics who would offer advice on one's love life or career. The psychics had big hair, and press-on fingernails. They smiled a lot, even when the news was not good.

And yes, my listeners, you see the purpose of this is two-fold—to gain perspective of the other, and to grow from the experience. You will see. In three months you will experience a shift toward the light.

"Toward the light?" the nervous caller repeats. "What, like... death?"

Again with the smile and the wobbly hair. "Perhaps a cruise...."

Perhaps a 169-day cruise, complete with gummy porridge or worse.

Letterman is chatting with a young actress who has found herself pregnant. It is okay, though, for she and her boyfriend have been dating over six months, and both really like kids.

Aris remembers the old televisions they had when she was growing up. The days of picture tubes. The way you'd click the set off and the picture would fade out slowly, Pioneer Letterman getting soft around the edges and then dulling out until he was a single dot on the screen.

Dunstan Regimbald seems surprised when she hands him the index card.

"What's this?"

"Tea. Or it would be if we were allowed to bring anything into this hermetically-sealed, CSI-swept room. It's down in my locker."

She has printed *Zhena's Gypsy Tea* neatly on the card.

"I'll get it for you later. It...."

"It's for tea time," his face breaks into the moon-faced smile.

That was painless, Aris shrugs. If only all her little encounters went that well. She is in an argument at work over, of all things, fridge space. Apparently leaving a large salad container on the middle rack is considered gauche, especially when one doesn't intend to share. No one mentions Lionel's medications, lined up neatly in the butter drawer. Nobody seems to have a problem with the temp's monster-sized diet soda. Probably mesmerized by her monster-sized….

Enough. *Genüg. Basta.*
Stop it, or you'll wind up like that girl, Maura Quell.

Who does Maura Quell end up as? What did her family say to scare *her*?

Genealogy. Aris didn't realize there would be this much math involved. She sees the faithful in the reading room, adding, subtracting, the *I've found him!* of one moment giving way to the sober reality of sums.

"No, see, Ingrid? He'd only have been seven. This is not him."

And that life is thrown back into the primordial ooze and another specimen of early ancestor is drawn forth. Ah, but this one has a different middle name and he lives in West Ham and not Norfolk. He lives in Connecticut and not Essen.

Bye-bye, Great Uncle Frederick.

Look at them. Who are these people who spend free days and evenings in the pursuit of dead people? Because when you find them, they are still dead.

"Look, he went to boarding school."
He is dead.
"Wow, she married so young. And look, a baby the following year."
She and the baby are dust.

📖

I told her it would come infected if she scratched and clawed at it. Now Caroline Lockett has a bandage on her ankle. I am afraid the wrapping is not clean. The ship's surgeon, Matthews, has told me to let the ankle to the air when Caroline is out on deck. He tells me for he believes her not only mute but insensible.

We have a game of pulling lice from one another's clothes and hair. It is a pitiful thing but it passes the time.

Midshipman Harkness has presented another shell. Does he travel with them? We are in blue water and I do not see where he is acquiring them. He is taken with Caroline. He could make an arrangement with someone, but he prefers this huge-eyed earnestness, and she has been known to walk with him a step or two.

It is maddening how she does not speak to him, for his eyes are full of questions. He looks to me to interpret, and I wish I could slap her hard on the arm and tell her to reply to him, herself.

Harkness is a gentleman, if such a thing exists on this vessel. I believe he is as happy to walk by her side, her ankle trailing a dirty swaddling rag, as comfort her in his bed.

What will happen when we reach Capetown? I have never heard or dreamt of such a place. Will my feet walk on land again? Surely Captain Ward will allow us to disembark, if only for the cleaning and provisioning. I do not know how many days or weeks ahead it is.

Cord says she has heard that the boy in the rigging, Marsh, has asked who I might be.

"I believe he has another." I say, for I have seen the one they call Jacobina in conversation with him. And she has disappeared from her rag-covered space from time to time.

"Biscuit," Cord mutters. "'T'aint no Ecckles cake. Mind, biscuit is better than nothing at all when you're hungry."

And I am hungry, so I walk away from her words. It is only when I am in bed later that I understand what she said.

"I took a shirt," I tell them. For the enormity and the pettiness of it round a corner in my mind and surprise me yet again. They are not listening to me.

"Pretty?" Caroline whispers, that strange voice gruff from lack of use.

Was it? Handsome? A man's shirt, trimmed with fine stitching. What had I wanted with it? Of all the things to steal.

"There was…there was so much lovely fabric. I could see our Eugene in a proper shirt, and me in a handkerchief or a light shawl. I think it seemed…so…wasteful."

She nods.

"And you?" I say quietly. "Inlaid hairbrush? Did you, in fact, purloin the Crown Jewels?" I put on my best proper voice.

She smiles and closes her pale, cracked lips.

Perhaps it was something else, something terrible. I see no direct violence in her ways. Nor is she the kind who would build upon her crimes to impress, like some.

"I killed my man."

"I was keeping rooms for ill intent."

"Burgled the tobacconist."

"Sneak thief."

And Caroline?

I lit a fire under the Landlord's window? I stole an Eccles cake from baker in back street?

And Herself speaking up.

"I took their pinnies. I had 'em shed, I did."

Caroline takes my hand as we lie in the bed. She holds it not as a chum, not a girl's gentle brushing of fingers. She holds it steady, as if she can see my intent.

They have found out that I can read and now the Bible is thrust upon me. I told them they had best be careful that it is not ripped up like the other one. But three are zealots in the ranks, as well, and they assure me that the Good Book, and myself, shall remain in one piece.

I do not mind quoting passages. It comforts some, and distracts others. It also allows me to sit somewhat apart from them which, in itself, is a blessing. We read about the Wedding Feast at Cana, and they all want a proper celebration after that. They talk about their marriages, their weddings to men they will probably never see again. Part of me is sorry for them. At least I had not begun my life. The ones who gave up children are not to be comforted. It is as it was on the day of our departure. And I ask myself how the Good Book can have this effect on the faithful.

My eyes long for another view. The horizon is blinding and unchanging, and I crave an imperfection, a blotch against the streak of colour. I should mind my thoughts because they believe there is weather on the way. The mates are busily battening and tying, tarring and lacing.

Marsh comes down from the rigging.

"You, there," he says. "Watch your step."

He says we will be sent down below shortly. Says he was listening while I read to the women.

"Who taught you to read like that?" he asks.

His hair is the colour of a rabbit in the woods.

"My mother."

He squints into the distance.

"Tell your mother she did good work, then."

Yes. Mother, even the ship's mates sing your praises.

The horizon closes in and we are told to go below. A few beg to stay on deck, but Captain Ward himself issues the order. The mates herd us up.

"Down ye go, Ladies. Mind yer 'eads."

Cord is next. Hanna. Maureen. Cassie Jukes shifts her odorous bulk and heaves it down the ladder, her gnarled hand the last piece of herself to disappear. And I see it, as clearly as if I'd done it, I see Caroline Lockett plant her foot on the exposed hand of Cassie Jukes.

Reading down below. They bring me a lantern and several await with the Book. One Book is whole, and cared for; the other, ripped to bits, makes up their infernal card game.

Cord says there are some players as have lost their shoes. This will prove poorly for them, she assures me. She is pleased that I can read, that, for a short time, I manage to keep the attention of this handful of women. So, I pick up the book, to Isaiah.

"Isaiah, Chapter 1, verse 16.

"Wash yourselves, make yourselves clean...."

—a groan from one of us, filthy and forgotten—

"...Put away the evil of your doings from before My eyes. Cease to do evil. Learn to do good...."

Rude comments from the game. A voice from Satan himself cackling in the timbers.

The ladies are not appreciative of this particular passage. I am about to switch to a psalm, when I see this, from Isaiah:

"And I will rid myself of My adversaries, and take vengeance on the enemies...."

Only the creaking now; everyone, even the card game, stops. Caroline Lockett, sitting up by the lantern, tightens her hand until it is a fist.

※

Aris's boss had smiled as he spoke of the increased workload over the next two weeks. The proceedings of an international symposium had to be summarized; there was a medical convention he'd be attending, along with the temp and her carry-ons. Sure enough, when Aris opened her Inbox, there was the entire proceedings. She always got these jobs producing fodder for the company library.

The temp...oh, she probably has a name...is calling a friend to cancel lunch. Aris can hear her voice as it wafts over the cubicle wall.

"No. No, I'm busy. We leave tomorrow. Yeah, through Philly."

A giggle.

The only thing worse than this would be hearing both sides of the conversation.

Aris hates symposium proceedings. She remembers the story about the symposium that was cancelled. The presenters had sent in their papers in advance, and the proceedings had been prepared. Somehow or other the proceedings were published, along with comments about the "stimulating discussion" the papers had generated along with the "wonderful response" from those attending the non-existent conference.

She would have to remember to tell Dunstan that one. Surely there were comparable library and archives stories.

Her orange chicken is not orange. It is the low-cal version, though, so perhaps that is why. She has not felt this sick in a dog's age. Nothing can cheer her up, not even the Dickens DVD package she'd been looking forward to, not even the card from the art gallery inviting her to another vernissage. She can hear kittens scurrying overhead. How many has the woman taken?

Free to a good home.

Somewhere atop my head.

This is beyond Tylenol, Aspirin, and the herbal teas. She has the bottle of gin from the summer's G&Ts.

Gin, the staple of the English Industrial Revolution. Cheap and available. Hadn't Dunstan quoted the old saying, "Drunk for a penny, dead drunk for two-pence?" Wicked on the throat, though. But add a little lemon, some hot water and honey and, there. Medicine.

She sips.

It's been a while since she's been to the library and archives. Maybe he's right. She could get a PC and sign up with an ancestry company. She could sit here in her pajamas, with her hot toddy, and do research. She would send in her DNA for analysis. And then get her company to let her work from home; the proceedings picked up in her Inbox. And she could order her food online and have it delivered, and…. And when she popped her clogs, kicked the bucket, took the long walk off that short pier, who in the world would know or care?

Wasn't there a real-life story about a man who died, sitting in front of his TV, only to be found years—years!—later, a skeleton with a remote control, the TV in darkness since the year the power had been cut?

That image had kept her up nights, and thoughts like that are what got her going to Dr. Grogan in the first place.

No. Maura will just have to wait for her to get back up and running. She'll just have to be a good girl and sit tight.

Four days later, and Aris is well enough to re-board the bus, the same bus that probably infected her. Maybe the seat-saver gave the bug to her, all downcast eyes and gentlemanly shuffle. *Here, take my seat.* Leaving behind his myriad sickly molecules.

Work is more bearable with the boss and the temp away. Doubtless they are exerting the same energy at the convention that they devote to their quality work here. Aris breezes through the morning, catching up on emails. She cleans out her rotting salad from the staff fridge. There is a post-it note on her container. It says: "EEEWWW!" in a childish hand, the same hand that is currently in Europe wrapped around something else that could probably use the post-it note.

Aris plans to leave at 3:00 so she can get to the library in time to catch Dunstan. He will be there until 5:00 or so. Aris doesn't mind working at night, normally. The trees outside the window are soothing when you can barely make out their silhouettes. They are just 'there.' She imagines that this is what it must have been like in the womb, when the various necessities—nutrition, oxygen, made their way to you. You were floating, and your baby brain was aware of sensations not entirely your own. The wavy world outside the window.

"He isn't here. Can I help you?"

Aris has little patience for staff. She really has to work on that.

"Is it his day off? I have something I'd like to...."

"He's not here. He's on a leave of absence."

Aris blinks. She is unaware of any leave of absence. He hasn't mentioned....

"Are you sure?"

Now it is the staff that should work on their patience.

A sigh, and then, "Are you a friend? Is this personal?"

Aris is stung by something. She feels herself getting red. Personal? Is it possible to be this flustered and this angry at the same time?

"Yes. Yes, he's a friend of mine. But I've been away."

Hasn't the woman seen her around the place? Doesn't she recognize her?

"He's helping me with a project but, yes, we're friends."

"Well...."

"Personal friends."

"I shouldn't say anything. But I have seen you here, and on break. Dunstan is in hospital."

"What?" Static from the carpet.

"He's okay. The surgery went well."

She stands at the bus stop, her bag of notes in one hand and the paper with the room number in the other. It starts raining lightly and the bus pulls up. She likes the sound of the wipers. She sits up front, in the seat-saver's normal spot.

Visiting hours. Lucky.

The desk is brightly lit. There is an empty cart by the elevator. A phone rings but nobody answers it.

Aris has always hated hospitals. She supposes that if one gave birth here, one might retain a happy memory. But for the rest of the populace hospitals are sad, sorry places. As a Canadian, she thanks her lucky stars and says the Tommy Douglas Prayer when she notes this, but still….

A cart of soiled laundry in the hall. A bucket. A metal tray with the remains of a meal. And a semi-private room with a white-haired man, asleep, in the bed by the door. Aris enters. A flat, moon-face, eyes closed, turned in the direction of the unopened window. A hospital gown of pale blue with tiny pink flowers all over it.

Sleeping. No tie. No vest, or bachelor pants. A mound in a bed, like all the other mounds. Aris sits in the chair beside him, pushing away the extra pillow. She hasn't done this, this hospital vigil, in years. Too painful, those memories, locked away with all other sadness of life.

So, in the present, in the here and now, she sits, looking at the quiet flow of the moon-faced man.

She dozes off thinking of Maura Quell, her time at the prison, her journey aboard the *Canada*. Sorry, Aris calls out to her, sorry it was the *Canada*. That's what we do, we Canadians. We say we're sorry.

"Aris?"

She jolts.

"Aris?"

Dunstan Regimbald is looking her way, a note of surprise in his voice.

"Uh…," she shakes herself alert. "Hi. Uh, hi. They told me you were here."

He nods, closes his eyes. Opens them.

"You know, there *are* other staff members who would assist you."

She is mortified until she notes the smile in his voice.

Yeah, well, I like to work 'em 'til they wind up in hospital," she smiles back.

"Dedication," he murmurs, and this is when she sees he is in pain.

"They said your surgery...."

"Yes. Fine."

She should be embarrassed. She should feel terrible sitting here with a man she hardly knows, a man who has just had his prostate removed.

"Uh...I know about hearts. Well, the organ, that is. Hearts, pacemakers, artificial hearts, stents, defibrillators. I don't know anything about this. Can I get you something?"

He shifts uncomfortably. "No. They'll be along soon. What time is it?"

Aris tells him. She has slept over half the visitor hours away.

"Yes, they'll be by with pills soon."

If she should feel awkward, well, so should he. Shouldn't he be thanking her, perfunctorily, and asking her to leave?

"They...they said only a few visitors. I don't want to take all the time...."

Dunstan's face has a silver glow when it looks to the window. He gestures with his hand around the room. As if on cue the old man in the other bed starts coughing.

"As you can see, I am, as they say, entirely at your disposal."

Aris glances at the old man. He has a greeting card by his bed. There is no card beside Dunstan's.

"I didn't know you were here, or I'd have brought a card or something. I went to the library. I've been sick, myself."

Is she trying to compare the flu to prostate cancer?

"So that's where you were. I'm sorry."

Does he think she's going to infect him?

"No, I'm fine now. Really."

"Have you been able to do anything on your project?"

"Well, I've been reading." Aris pulls out a book, grateful for the change of topic. "Conditions. Sailing dates. Life on board ship." She retrieves a description from the book and starts reading. She stops.

"Does it bother you if I read this?"

A half-hour passes and visitors are told it is time to leave. Dunstan suggests a couple of leads for Aris to consider. She stands and notices she is grimacing.

"Hang on."

She races to the main desk.

"My friend…. Mr. Dunstan Regimbald in 28B requires his pain medication," she says in her most officious voice.

The nurse doesn't even look up.

"I said…."

"She's on the floor. Patients will get their meds when visitors leave."

Aris hurries back.

"She's…coming. And I have to go."

Dunstan reaches his hand over to hers but she has to come part way. She notices his fingernail cuticles, pure as any baby's, like little quarter-moons.

"It was nice of you to visit," he says simply.

There is a bit of a wait for the bus, so Aris sits out on a bench. The sky is clear now, and dark, the moon and the stars visible above the outline of the buildings. The populace exits to cars and the bus lineup, people who have spent this evening of their lives sitting, or standing, by a bed, or doing the slow-motion walk through the halls, or begging a loved one to eat.

Back at home, Aris rubs the back of her neck and rolls her head. This is when she misses a husband. Or a paid servant. She thinks over the day. How it had been planned and how the plan went to hell. How she left the library and went over to the hospital. She thinks of poor Dunstan Regimbald, his body healing from this drastic change. She can only imagine the things going through his head, how this will affect and complicate his life. Nobody his age gets prostate cancer. It's so rare it's crazy. Does he have anybody to help him? She has never even asked if he has a girlfriend. She has suspected not, but she has been wrong about stuff like this before.

She should offer to help. But how? Aris puts on some Erik Satie, low so she can barely hear it, more like she is listening to it through a window, like someone is playing the music down the road and she can hear it.

It is strange to witness the decline of Hettie Rags Crenshaw. There was a time she might have controlled much of this world below deck. In Newgate she had a long reach, and skivvies to take on her intent. She walked with purpose then; now she hobbles, and there are no disciples in her wake.

All the while, Cassie Jukes grows stronger. The gaming, the rum totes gambled off people, or stolen, the favours she requires and allows. She is the maker of such a place.

That I should feel pity for Hettie Crenshaw shows how far she has fallen. That I should locate her shoe after it's been tossed by one of Cassie's skrags is strange to me.

Maura Quell, are you minding yourself? Are you keeping yourself out of harm's way?

Yes, Mother. For now.

It is a lesson, I am sure, to see someone dwindle. To see the spirit leave the eyes, as one watches a person being bled. Her bold cackle, her swooping into a crowd, gone. She who could once pick your pocket while you stood by a shop, she who had them running about doing her bidding, she is now a carved thing, her features wearing down in the salt rain.

Cassie Jukes shrieks. Another prize from another hapless soul.

Why has she never come after Caroline Lockett for crushing her hand on the ladder? Thought it was a ship's mate? And better to leave it at that?

Harkness has put a hole in one of the shells and Caroline wears it now on a string about her neck. I told her that I once wore a tiny seahorse skeleton until I realized it was rotting. Harkness heard me and laughed. He has an open, manly laugh.

"Don't you want to talk to him?" I ask her when we are scrubbing filth from plates.

Not that I wish her to leave me for his bed, but at least to say his name. Does he deserve at least that much?

I realize how badly I want to know why she cannot, will not, speak.

"Was it something terrible?"

"Is your innocence dependent on your silence?"

"Are you afraid of someone, Caroline?"

I feel a terrible thing must have happened to her. I know of no other reason for her to maintain this stone-like silence. We are a long way from England—we are approaching the Line, they say.

I have heard rumours of wild, drunken terrors there, hideous spectacle at the Equator, with none among us safe. I look to Midshipman Harkness and see a reasonable man. How can the stories be true? Initiation for sailors? Rituals? I hear of everyone being forced into the event. I shall try to hide if this is the case. I shall take Caroline and I shall hide.

Trying to think back to the history I was creating for her, back in Newgate. It seems a life ago.

O, Maura, it was a life ago. But whose? Not Caroline's. Who were you to state her story?

I know, Mother. Always the fanciful one. But she had no story and it seemed that this was the worst manner in which to endure the prison, without stones or mortar or anything to hold one steady.

I, Maura Quell, had you, Mother. Had our Eugene, and the home near the forest, had Mary Lavender and the rabbits in the field. Had the word, on the page, to read in the evening. And the tree over your shoulder, outside the window.

How could I wish for less for Caroline? So I started her story. I never expected to have to change it. And yet, has it not changed? She tells me nothing and yet I know that there are no parents to grieve for her, just as there were non to appeal on her behalf. There is no home to go back to when our time is up. Without any words, I know that she and I are the same, two sea birds perched on this vessel, without home or family. Two people who are free.

It begins. I have heard it lasts two days. Cord has been told to gather such food and refreshments as can be bartered or scrimped. The crew is preparing their part in this. They have every intention of taking over the vessel. My stomach churns as I see the vile concoction they are mixing in vats on deck. The stench is exceedingly bad.

Caroline stays close as we observe the enlisted men, like Marsh, make their own preparations. They will attack the officers. Harkness is over with another midshipman. They talk as they make their rounds, and I see a smile, but both are glancing fore and aft and are walking with uncommon briskness.

The ritual is to reverse the established order of things. It is to allow chaos and disarray to reign. So says Cord. And I am wondering whether this existence can become any more disordered.

Cord looks at Cassie Jukes and her lot and gives us unspoken direction to stay out of the way. She says that there is much drinking on deck. We can hear the shouts. The hatch has been opened and many of the women are now on deck as well. Cord goes up.

Caroline looks at me.

"Want to go?" she asks.

I know, Mother. I am a fool. But part of me wants to know what is occurring up there.

The tars have control of the ship. Midshipman Harkness has his hair pulled loose. He has been ordered to holystone the deck, which he is doing more good-naturedly than other officers are enduring their 'punishment.' One midshipman is in the rigging and the surgeon is getting a shave from a young sailor. Upon closer examination I see it is Marsh who is doing the honours.

Cassie Jukes is holding forth from a coil of rope. She has obtained a flask and is drinking from it, cursing and singing all manner of song.

Caroline taps my hand and leads me over to where mates are opening a large fish, I know not what kind. The air fills with a curious reek and our eyes widen as we see the man hollow out the fish and then wrap it round his leg, like a garter. There is seaweed on deck, slimy and intensely green. Caroline taps again and we are over to where more liquid and foul brine are being swirled together.

I eat something from a hand, some kind of salt meat, and drink from a cup.

How I got to my hammock, I do not know. I awaken in a guttering lantern-light to see lumps, bags of flesh poured into their beds, arms and legs splayed as if they have been dropped from a great height. Caroline's spot is empty. There is not much noise up on deck.

I rise, holding my head, which seems to sway. My stomach and bowels could relieve themselves at any moment, so I move carefully to the slop bucket. Afterward, with a hand out to steady the beams, I make my way up the ladder.

It is a clear morning. The sun is the horizon, is the whole sky. We are crossing the equator.

All are up for the trial. I recognize King Neptune as the first mate, Byers, though he is much transformed, the silver flash of scales draping his body, a seaweed cape or scarf dripping from his arms. His face has been painted with something so as to make him look entirely of the netherworld, and if I did not know who he was he would frighten me.

I see Marsh and the other initiates. They are to be interrogated for their part in the uprising. Whereas there was a good deal of jostling and laughter yesterday, the faces on the initiates, this day, betray unease.

Cord said it was a ritual known to all sailors who cross the Equator. But the rituals vary, they say, and none of these men know, for certain, what will befall them. One of the mates, Groot, or somesuch, has a look of cockiness, and so he is the first to be interrogated. They ask foolish questions for which he has no answers. They demand his involvement in yesterday's chaos.

Midshipman Wickenham points to Groot. "He's the one. He had me up in the rigging doing repair."

Groot is stood before the King. He is stripped of his shirt and his head is dunked in a barrel of that vile bilge grog they put together. He sputters, gags, is sick and is put in again. I am afraid he might choke. He emerges and is sat on the stool. His head is covered with fish entrails.

Marsh. O, Marsh.... He looks my way just as they dunk him in. His arms are perfectly still behind his back; he neither fights nor flails. Three times they dunk him, for good measure. He must run barefoot across fish guts and excrement, and falls several times.

In the end, all the initiates are side by side before the king. Neptune rises. He holds out his makeshift trident and thunders:

"These beings…that have disrupted the natural order and that have not given me my due as King of this realm, these beings should be keelhauled."

A shudder runs across the desk.

"However, as I am both benevolent and wise, and bearing in mind the tithe I will expect of every one of them, I am prepared to demand, instead, that these filthy, reeking specimens be made fit for their return to duty. They will, therefore, be put over the side!"

A whoop goes up as the hapless men, Marsh included, are dragged to the ropes that have been fitted at the stern. I do not go back to see them being thrown overboard. I have heard that one can lose men this way and do not want to witness that.

Cries and shouts of "watch him!" and "hang on!" continue for some time until the men are brought up, and they collapse on deck. A general cheer is roused for these newest, seasoned sailors. Their ordeal is over. On their next voyage, it will be someone else. I walk back in time to see Marsh being helped to his feet. He is handed his shirt and a flask.

I am told we will be cleaning up today, swabbing all this muck off the ship. We have Crossed the Line, says Cord.

Where is Caroline? I am about to go to the Surgeon to inquire when she appears on deck. Her head is down as she scrubs a stair.

"Caroline," I run to her. She looks up. Her face is the same but there is something in her face. She nods and is about to set her eyes back on her work.

"Where were you? Are you well?"

She nods and scrubs.

And then I know it. She was gone with him. With Midshipman Harkness.

❈

Did she stop in Capetown, or Rio? Did they let her off the *Canada* to walk the unfamiliar soil?

Aris is supposed to be finishing the proceedings, but she is staring at the picture of the Rose Bowl Parade, tacked onto her cubicle wall. All those flowers, lovely in the photo, trampled within a day.

She is going to see Dunstan tonight. He has been moved to the Rehab Centre, proof of her theory that there is no one to care for him at home. The bachelor pants, the in-depth knowledge of movie times and dates, the precise inventory of the ingredients in certain pre-fab food items, confirmation.

"I'll have to start back slowly. I won't be in work full-time for a while."

Why does this irritate Aris? Surely she can't begrudge the man his recovery.

"Skiving," she mutters to herself as she gets back to work, herself.

The boss will be back after the weekend and will expect the office to be running like a well-oiled guillotine.

Detecting during a scheduled angiogram can result in the opportunity to correct....

I serve the heart.

The thought slaps her. This is what she does—she spends her waking hours in the service of this mindless organ.

Heart.

Description: pump.

She stops by the flower shop after work and chooses a small mixed bouquet. The woman asks if she wants it gift-wrapped but Aris says no. It is strange enough to be doing this without the addition of bows. How long has it been since anyone brought her flowers? Derek used to, in the early days. Then it was half a bag of pretzels or a coupon for discount pizza.

This evening Dunstan is walking. He wears a striped robe and felt slippers and he looks like a large elf, one of Santa's bouncers. He moves like an old man, though.

"How many laps?" she asks.

He looks up, grimacing. "Here to the nurse's desk. And back."

"Don't quit your day job. Need any help?"

He waves her off so Aris goes to locate a vase. At least, she hopes it's a vase and not one of those things men pee in. She arranges the flowers, plucking off a deadhead.

"Nice," he says, and lowers himself slowly into his chair.

"Sit," he nods, meaning the bed. Aris perches.

Glasses! He is putting a finger to the bridge of his nose to straighten invisible glasses. Does he even know they're missing? Without them, his face is even rounder, and radiates silver. Aris reaches over to the bedside table and retrieves the glasses.

"So, show me your spoils."

Aris spreads out the chart she's been making, containing images of ships, printout information, drawings of below-deck, 'tween-deck, masts.

"Interesting," Dunstan says. "So, where is our girl now?"

They have begun calling her that. Maura Quell. Aris started it, quite innocently. "Well, come on, my girl, what are you up to?" It is almost her grandmother's voice when she says it. Dunstan must have picked up on it. Did he pick up on the Poignant Moment as well, the sight of two childless people, one prostateless, one menopausal, examining charts and lists, in search of their little girl?

Dunstan congratulates her on her efforts.

"You have a date to work with at the other end. You have to start working from that end, looking for her over there."

"But...."

In her mind, Maura Quell is still on the boat. She is only partway to her destination. But that makes no sense. She isn't anywhere.

"I keep thinking I'll find her."

Dunstan nods. "I know. I see it all the time. It's like if only I connect all the dots, they'll walk through that door. I've told my colleagues at work that maybe these researchers are the Gen R virtual gamers. I mean, how can it get more virtual—you put in the numbers, the reference names, and out comes a real person? An avatar of your very own."

"Do...you think of it as a game?"

Dunstan's track pants are bachelor track pants. "Me? No. A puzzle, yes. A game, never."

Dunstan goes over the *Canada*'s information.

"Given the year, her age when arriving, and the location, you might be looking at servant, or a prisoner at Parramatta. At the Female Factory."

"The what?"

"Female Factory. Look it up," he says, and shifts awkwardly in his seat.

All the way home on the bus the words trip her up. They sound like something out of a horror movie. Night buses on Fridays are funny. Young, careless couples on dates, old Chinese men with a week's worth of groceries on their laps, the occasional boozehound reeking of scotch or gin. One well-dressed, crazy woman is talking to...no...disagreeing with herself. She is making a good case and getting the upper hand...then when she turns Aris sees the Bluetooth pacifier in her ear.

The bus as office.

The coffee shop as office.

The office as dating pool.

Thank God it's Friday.

It comes to Aris that this is precisely the kind of moment that precipitated the coinage of that phrase. Some poor slob drifting home on the winds of a Friday night, and too many idiots on the bus.

Aris makes no apologies to anyone for the flannel PJ pants and the Heart Institute conference t-shirt.

"So, sue me," she calls out to the forensic specialist on TV. She flattens the cardboard chart she's been working on, the information log. She writes: "Our girl. Parramatta?" She will go to the archives tomorrow to follow up on it. She'll pick up a magazine for Dunstan on the way over to rehab. She heard him talking sports with the technician once. Something sporty.

Aris lies in her bedroom cubicle. Work cubicle, bedroom cubicle, little cubicle in the funeral parlour. Bleak stuff for a Friday night. It would be nice to have a lost evening. A bar with good music, okay, maybe too loud, but listenable music. In graduate school she knew the DJ at the local bar. He'd see her there and would play her favourite tunes. Ensconced behind his equipment, he never said more than a hello, but he always played something for her.

Some nights there were friends from classes, fellow poli-sci, or English grad people, the occasional physicist sitting through the ass-end of an experiment.

"I have to check it in two hours."

One of the bartenders fundraising for the IRA.

The drama people would arrive. Someone would get up to dance the strange dances of the 80s. Aris, on occasion, would be persuaded by one of the drama crew to stand up and gyrate on the very rim of the microscopic dance floor before her partner would morph into Carmen Miranda or start channelling Frank N. Furter. They would dance the Time Warp with energy and egos and Aris would glance over at the DJ, who would smile.

Enough crazy energy. Enough pseudo-disco. Enough wine, and perhaps a friend to take home for the evening. It was foolish and fond. It was unreal and yet, lying in her bedroom cubicle, Aris knows it was more real than her years with Derek, than the garage with its gardening tools never touched. Than the child they never had.

Parramatta. A plot of land. Something called Experiment Farm.

When. *When* you are there seems to matter. Maura Quell arrives in 1810. By then the original buildings have burnt back down to the Parramatta grass. There is a jail, a gaol, a "factory" for females. They work there, live there; or they get farmed out as servants to the local landowners. Or they get taken in marriage.

Taken in marriage? Lined up and paraded before the populace. Even children. Even girls like Maura? Servants. Wives. Prisoners. Aris reads and cross-references. Is she married off? Is she the servant to someone only slightly higher on the ladder than she? Is she an inmate of the factory?

Aris. Wait. She is still on the boat, isn't she?

Dunstan is hoping to borrow a laptop from Bruce, the technician.

"He's afraid someone will abscond with it. I'll put it down to go to therapy and someone will rip it off."

Aris glances around. "I guess it's possible."

"Not if it's chained to my wrist….Yeah, I know. I don't exactly look like Bond. But, on the upside, they've removed the catheter."

Too much Dunstan Regimbald information. Aris can only nod.

Dunstan invites her along for the mandatory stroll down the hall.

📖

What has he done to Caroline Lockett? Her stomach hurts so. She is bound up, and they have administered elixir vitriol to loosen her bowels. She moans. I visit with her, but the surgeon says there is nothing to do but wait until nature takes its course. I hold her hand. The shell on the string about her neck floats upon her breast, a wave on the ocean, such waves as we have not.

We have been in the doldrums these many days. Our feet are roasted on deck. The tar seams soften and they burn. They burn through the soles of these poor shoes. Eugene would not have any shoes; it is good that he is not here. O, Maura Quell. It is good that he is gone? What does that say of a life, that it is good that he is not in it?

Caroline groans.

"Caroline," I squeeze her hand.

Midshipman Harkness came by to see her. He stood off and spoke with the surgeon. He asked about pain medications. The surgeon complained about the filth, the bilge and the black water. For it is truth that we need the wind to outrun our own filth. We are mired in ourselves, in our own foul cesspool.

Caroline sleeps again, so I go above deck. I have taken a sleeve from my dress and fashioned a kerchief, but my eyes are nearly blinded by the ball of fire overhead.

Marsh is trying to contain tar in places, a hot and hopeless job. He sees me and puts his fingers to his cap, the way he salutes his captain. But I am no captain. I nod and make my way over to where Cord is trying to separate grain from whatever else has gotten into it.

Would that Maura Quell were a saint and could live on the Body of Christ alone, like those holy ones in times past who slowly gave up on eating, subsisting on water and the Holy Spirit.

But, alas, I am no saint; no more than I am the captain.

Maura Quell, are you behaving yourself? Mind you do.

I shall, Mother. But even you, Mother, at your most obedient, would not wish to be picking mealworms or somesuch out of a bowl.

The sea is a blue plate. We could serve crumpets on it, dripping in honey or butter. We could lay the table with the tatted cloth from your wedding, Mother. We could get some cream from Darcy's lane.

"You. Back to work."

Cord's patience as thin as the eyelids of a saint.

When I return to the surgeon's I find Caroline Lockett sitting up. A weak tea or broth is beside her and she looks altogether less beset. The surgeon wishes me to look after her when she returns below deck.

I'm happy to see, when I later help her to her feet, that she has been given a fresh bandage with some unguent on it, tied about her ankle.

"You caused me a scare," I tell her.

I am shorter but my shoulders are a support. She leans on me as we hobble out.

Hettie Rags Crenshaw is a heap in the corner. Cord is happy to see Caroline. She makes sure Caroline is put to bed, her garments loosened, and she wipes her forehead with a dry cloth.

By evening Caroline is up and about, and she eats a bowl with me. We sit and listen as Cassie Jukes breaks another one, a woman who's played cards with her and who now is debt to her. The poor one is scrubbing the floor at Cassie's feet while Her Ladyship rests her own obscene pegs on the woman's back.

I believe that there is such a thing as pure hatred. That it is pure; that it is as hot and white as that ball of fire over our heads.

We are allowed up on deck, but there is no relief. Someone is singing and there is a squeeze-box. It is homey and mournful all at once. The nameless tune reminds all of us that once, a lifetime ago, we were not in this state, on this ship, stranded in this solid water.

Caroline edges over. Sits, eyes on the reaches of the horizon.

"You can go blind like that," I tell her.

Harkness is on watch and stops by as he makes his way. He smiles at Caroline, and he smiles at me. He is, perhaps, a gentleman. I wish to ask her. I have so many questions. But tonight in this endless heat and sun there is only the tune playing, and my thoughts cannot get beyond that, and the deck, and Cassie Jukes consorting with a toothless tar.

Caroline sleeps beside me, exhausted. I watch her face by the dim lantern light. She is lovely. She would be lovely. In my history of Caroline Lockett, she wore that dress to a concert in the square. Her hair, straw now…there…it's out of your face…her hair was…plaited? And she pressed a chain with a cross, or a locket, like her name, to her breast, not a shell that reeks of these far waters.

And in the night, O, Miracle! And in the night a wind that comes from the lungs of God, and a rain that thunders down upon us, rupturing through holes caused by the shifting chinks and bubbled tar. Buckets, laughter, up on deck and down below. Drenched to the skin, our clothes shredding, flames guttering, and much yelling barely heard over the cracking of the skies.

By the time it passes, we are sodden masses, but we are moving again, wind in our sails. Marsh is top-mast; he looks like a fine bird perched atop a cathedral steeple.

I have told Cord about it. I have spoken and been cuffed by one of Her Ladyship's skivvies. What she gets up to is beyond tolerance. Now she has the poor ones serving her like she's the Queen of Sheba.

She beats the young one, Izzy Watts. I say young, but she is the same age as Caroline and me.

"Whatzit?" as Cassie Jukes has branded her, is a broken egg, a punched-in hat. Which makes her fair game for the others.

"Every kinchin mort should 'ave the very same, n'all," Cassie Jukes struts. And Whatzit jerking around behind her, lifting up the filthy train in her wake.

So it is no surprise when they find the girl rolled up in her bindle.

"She's rowed her way up Barmy River, that one," they whisper.

The Surgeon gives her a dose of laudanum. If there was a fit house on board, she would be in it.

There are grumblings and more over this. Cord tells us all to stay calm and let it pass.

"How much worse for her is it now?" Cord says, almost wishing for the same stupor, I believe. And, in truth, how much more can I hate Cassie Jukes?

It is when I see her at night, over in the corner with her infernal card game. When I see her looking for the next one, priming the next one stupid enough to want to join her party.

Caroline has been gone two nights, but now she returns to me. We keep our voices low as we whisper about Izzy Watts. And it is not too long before we come up with a plan.

✺

It is Dunstan's first day back home from rehab. The nurse was dismissive when Aris called, saying that he had been discharged and offering no further information.

Why does this surprise her? As a member of no official party, whom does she think she represents? Aris finds herself lifting her salad leaves with even less enthusiasm than usual. The boss and the temp are back. The temp is managing to cause Aris to hate Australians.

"Treena" is abnormally tanned. At least Steve Irwin spent time outside. Treena lives in salons and shopping malls, a strange mutant that alters her pigment to suit her dress.

Why is it unusual that Aris would look up his address in the phone book? Is this how stalkers begin? And how many Regimbalds had she expected to find? There's only the one, D. Regimbald. Of course he lives in an area it will take her two bus switches to get to.

Carrying a meatloaf on the bus is depressing, but there it is. At least, on this unpopular bus route, there is room to sit. People, hungry people, are eyeing her parcel. The Google Map stop is three or more blocks from his residence. Does he do this everyday?

Yes, Aris, but he is not carrying a meatloaf and boiled potatoes in a bag. She must look like she's carrying the prehistoric version of those boil-in-the-bag convenience foods, the early prototype complete with awkward lumps and escaping heat. Shit.

Drab part of town, ghosting the river. At one time it might have been nice, but now it's dusty dog paths and graffiti-covered storage units. Equally drab apartment block, a post-war institutional initiative. Only eight units, though, like her apartment building.

She sees his name beside the dented mailbox. She rings REGIMBALD.

Nothing.

REGIMBALD.

What an idiot idea this was. This is why they invented the telephone. Alexander Graham Bell saw idiots like her standing in front halls with steam coming out of their bags. If she didn't want to wake him with the phone, what is she doing now, at the door?

A buzz. Aris races up, grabs the handle and pulls just as the buzz stops. The door opens. Absurd to feel this victorious. The hallway is dark and smells like beefy books. A lock is undone down the hall. Aris approaches. A half-moon appears around the door frame.

"Aris?"

He sounds completely surprised. Why is he so completely, absolutely, shocked to see her here?

Well, Stalker #5, perhaps it's because he's an employee of the archives and not your long lost brother. Perhaps it's because you come bearing a meal, like a comfort-food Welcome Wagon serial-killer....

"How did you know where I live?" he asks, stepping aside to let her in.

"Oh, you know. Advanced genealogical skills. I checked the phone book."

"Pardon the mess," he says half-heartedly, for she can see that in his current state there is little he can do about picking up after himself.

The apartment is smaller than hers and less bright as well. But she can see that, except for recent untidiness, it is generally well kept. She finds the kitchen and puts the food into the oven to reheat. Then she returns to the living room where she has left him standing, holding her jacket.

"I thought you might like a meal," she says.

He walks slowly and takes a seat. He has an afghan on his chair, which he wraps around himself.

"Sit," he says," if you can find a spot."

The couch has a comforter and a pillow and Aris is uncomfortable siting on what is obviously a day bed, so she walks around looking at books on the shelves and photos on the mantel.

A lovely period photo of a young girl with curly hair, a lacy dress and a hair bow.

"My grandmother," he reads her mind.

Aris nods. The room embodies solitude. But he has a couple of cards up, one with a dog holding a saw. The dog has a human grin.

"Pardon my asking," he says, "but don't you have anywhere else to be?"

He blushes as soon as he says it, for apparently it has come out wrong. Apparently the intent hasn't been to embarrass Aris to the roots of her tinted hair.

"Ah, God, I hate these painkillers. I lose what little where-with-all I have. I meant that it's really nice of you to do this. I would assume that someone like you has far better things to do with her time."

Aris is still recovering from the opening salvo.

"It smells very good," Dunstan adds, jerking his head back toward the kitchen.

By the time they finish eating, Dunstan is tired. He has tried to stay up for the recommended amount of time but finds that he needs frequent rests.

"I'll go," Aris almost jumps.

"No...no, I don't mean go," he says. "I'm just going to lie down here, if that's okay. You can stay. Tell me a story. I feel just about helpless and small enough to need a story right about now."

He stretches out on his long couch and pulls the comforter over him. This leaves Aris with the chair. She moves the afghan, sits, and looks across at the prone body of Dunstan Regimbald, and the kapock-stuffed sarcophagus of a medieval knight.

She doesn't know any stories. Her life of imaginative stories ended when her parents crashed their Impala and their heads on the way to the CNE.

"I don't have any stories," she murmurs.

"Sure you do. Anything without catheters or diapers will be fine."

Aris thinks. Fiction is not possible for her. Her entire life is facts; even this genealogy is an attempt to explain the world through facts.

"So," she starts, as Dunstan draws up the covers. "Let me tell you a story, a true story, about the man who invented the artificial heart."

"Jarvik," Dunstan says.

"No."

Aris sees the eyes open.

"No. The first guy who invented it."

And she begins the story of the ventriloquist, of Paul Winchell, and his enormous talent. Of the little wooden dummies. Of a dance contest on the "Arthur Murray Dance Party" TV show and Winchell's chance meeting with Henry Heimlich, Arthur Murray's son-in-law.

"Heimlich, as in Maneuver?"

"Same."

Of Paul Winchell conversing with Dr. Heimlich, observing operations.

"This friend of his, Doctor Foreman, thought it was sad that these people were dying on the table while their hearts were being repaired. And how cool it would be if they could have another, temporary, heart to do the pumping."

Dunstan is leaning toward her. He looks uncomfortable.

"This is Jarvik," he insists.

"Lie down, you'll hurt yourself," Aris demands. "And, I told you, this is pre-Jarvik."

Dunstan slumps back.

"Like I said, before I was so rudely interrupted, Winchell comes up with the idea. The doc tells him that since he's so good at building the wooden dummies for his act, why doesn't he build the first artificial heart? So he...."

"You're telling me a ventriloquist built the first artificial heart?"

"Not just any ventriloquist. He was also the voice of Tigger in *Winnie the Pooh*."

Dunstan clicks dismissively.

"Don't believe me? Google it. You know what the weirdest part is? I'll always remember it. Know what Winchell said about it? He said that building the heart wasn't that different from building a dummy."

The sun is setting against Dunstan Regimbald's dusty windows. She notices, for the first time, a tired-looking plant in the corner. It's small, an eight-inch pot. It has been totally neglected.

"I'm going to water the plant, okay?"

"Sure...what plant?"

Aris takes the pot—is it a pepper plant?—into the kitchen and gives it a good drenching in the sink. Once she is sure it has drained she wipes the leaves and cleans the saucer beneath.

"There," she tells the nameless barely-living thing. She brings it back into the living room and puts it on the shelf.

Dunstan Regimbald has fallen asleep. He looks like a child, there, his precise fingernails, his glowing face.

Aris puts the leftovers in the fridge. Bachelor fridge. Milk, a six-pack of eggs, some half-used bottles of condiments. She lets herself out, making sure the door is on automatic lock. The beef smell is gone from the hall. There is only the book smell now.

As she waits for her bus she remembers how Winchell was laughed out of the American Medical Association, and how the University of Utah finally acquired his patent. By the time Barney Clark received the first artificial Jarvik heart, Winchell's contribution was largely forgotten.

But Aris can see him at home in his studio, fashioning a heart while his wooden dummies look on, and they knowing that he will be able to make it work because he has breathed life into all of them as well.

It is this image that first brought her to the heart. The picture of a man, a comedian, really, a clown with a dummy, a man who would one day sing about Tiggers, creating something that is not even human, but something that is called a heart.

Heart.

Function: to pump, to circulate, blood.
       to ache and yearn
       to spill with joy

Spill? Too graphic.

       to brim with joy

"That's right, Dr. Grogan. I've been caring for a friend."

Aris is sure Dr. Grogan has a chart of her life, with little boxes checked off:

Friend—4 points

Caring—4 points

"You're doing so well, Aris!"

Caring—5 points?

Dr. Grogan wants to see more of this selfless involvement. On the whole, though, he feels she has come along so exceptionally that he recommends scheduling down on her appointments.

"Something less regular," he says. "More of a pit stop, if you will." He smiles.

Another one of his word pictures. Aris pulling in, in a Formula One precision automobile, and Dr. Grogan seeing to all her needs in seconds.

After heating an instant dinner, Aris sits at the counter listening to the two—no, three?—cats gamboling above her. Has the woman taken *all* the cats? Aris pours the pasta onto a plate, refusing to eat from the container. What kind of fraud is it to call this stuff food? The proof will be a hundred years from now, when the Rapture happens and all the people from this generation arise with full bodies intact, nothing biodegraded, but everyone that sickly colour of fake cheese. There'll be a W5 episode about it, and Aris will be a guest for the "Big Reveal", as Oprah calls it, and Aris's

105

preserved corpse will send somebody to prison for something unnatural.

Prison brings her back to the folder in her bag. She has been busy this week. She's neglected her work. She's also neglected Maura Quell.

How is it that we speak without words? Caroline does so always, but now I realize that I also do this, communicate without speaking. I am learning from her. She tells me not to fear Marsh if he comes for me. The bounty of being the choice of a mate is not that which it is with a midshipman, but she holds the shell in her long hand and twirls it as she ponders the horizon.

He has not come. I think this is my own disagreeableness, and the filth, of course. But he has not offered. He smiles at me from his post and I nod back.

Caroline has visited the broken Izzy Watts. She has heard the evening card games, the threats. I am sure that she hates Cassie Jukes every bit as much as I do.

"Get on with it," Cord instructs, as I kneel into my work with the scrub brush.

Caroline comes back because of me. I know this. She has a better situation with Harkness, but she returns to me. I feel it in her hand, when she reaches for mine. How long since the trials? Fetid Newgate? The boiled face of the guard staring at us?

Now we are to rip a damaged cloth into rags, kerchiefs, to be used in the clinic. I expected this to be hard work, but the cloth fairly falls apart in our fingers. Caroline puts one over her head and creates a grand turban that, even in these conditions, makes her appear noble.

I curtsy. We laugh. I wrap one round my head and I am an old woman hobbling about, a bird woman in a town square. All I am missing is the crumbs in my apron.

Now she is a maiden, her face covered below the eyes. She is hooded and mysterious. She looks for all the world to be a princess from a far-off land. I pause to consider. Who knows who she is, really? And we are from a far-off land, are we not?

Cassie Jukes has someone braiding her matted hair. She is complaining and hitting out every time a knot is discovered. I should like to place ants in her mass of tangles. They would be eaten by whatever lives in there, I am sure.

"Oy, you."

She is pointing my way.

"One of them bindle rags for me."

I look at the cloth.

"They're for the clinic," I reply.

"Don't cuss me, Missie. Pass it over."

I shake my head.

"You—"

She smacks the arm of the one braiding her hair.

"—go get me a kerchief."

The eyeless wonder approaches. Caroline stands up, as do I.

"These are for another use," I tell her. She, as blindly, turns round.

"You give me," Cassie Jukes threatens.

The bewitched one turns again.

"No," I say, leaving the stricken one stranded in the middle.

Now it is Cassie Jukes rising with a groan. She rearranges her rotting garments and approaches. The smell is terrible.

"Your pretty little ears ain't working? Maybe we'll jest take one of 'em off then, eh?"

Before she can make her move, Caroline Lockett has come between us, her tall form blocking my view.

"Push off," I hear her gruff, boy voice.

I stand, blind, my ears open.

"Oh! You…ye kin speak! Sh…she kin speak!"

Cassie Jukes is surprised enough to let down her guard. Caroline kicks out at her hand, and for the first time I see the shiny blade. There's a clink as it drops to the deck.

108

I have to say that I do not understand why I do it, but I pick up the offending weapon and race to the side and throw it mightily overboard. When I turn back I see that Cassie Jukes has recovered herself and has Caroline down. She is stepping on her bad ankle.

I fly to her, landing on the witch's back. She whirls around like a dog chasing its tail. I cling like a cat to a tree and I remember a little twist Eugene used to make me turn left or right when he was on my back. I pull her newly braided hair until she shrieks, and she is off Caroline.

One more jerk and I am off her and I turn to face her.

But her bulk is her enemy and she has gone down. Her minions help her and pick up her bits and bobs as have fallen or been torn from her clothes. She is speechless, as if Caroline's affliction has passed to her. But her eyes are speaking. She, too, can speak without words, and she is saying things I would never say aloud.

She limps away and I go back to Caroline

"She has it in for us now, I'm afraid," Caroline winces. The ankle is opened up and I can see when she removes the bandages that the infection has never really gone away. I beg a mate for a bucket of sea-water, which I use to wash the sore. I take two rags from the pile and bind her ankle, all the while Cassie Jukes watching from afar.

We have fallen into it now, I know. There will be no more proper resting from here on. Caroline could go to Harkness. She could stay with him.

"I won't leave you," she says, as if by some magic she can now read my deepest mind.

The first night neither of us sleeps. It is hard to keep our eyes open but we whisper over many things. She likes Harkness. He is a man of many talents. He is hot and cold. He is hard and soft.

"He thinks me suitable," she says, and I am seeing, in my mind, her mouth speaking the words but hearing, in my ears, the raspy young boy's voice.

Cassie Jukes means to tire us. She bides her time. I tell Caroline that we must be more clever, which we both agree can't be too difficult. But Cassie Jukes has those as would do things for her, and we do not know everyone in her militia. So we keep to ourselves as much as possible.

Caroline says she will stay with me and not return to Harkness until she is sure Cassie Jukes cannot harm us.

"She wants your guts for garters," she says.

"My eyeballs for unguent," I say back, daring her.

"Your spleen for sport," she says.

And I cannot decide which bit of me should go next.

We make our way up past the 'tween-deck to catch the breeze on deck.

Midshipman Harkness is commanding the boson, who in turn is piping to the men. Someone in the forecastle lets out a holler and then Cord yells, "Look!"

We all look to see sharks at the starboard side.

Hungry, they are, and we like little delicacies on plates, fine white lawn napkins at our sides. The pod has been following us, we hear. Someone else says it was dolphins yesterday. Marsh laughs and says there's quite a difference between sharks and dolphins.

You see, Mother? I am learning.

O Maura, didn't I say it was better to know than not to know? To be able to read is a wonderful gift.

Yes, Mother. So is knowing a dolphin from a shark.

I spend much of the morning imagining myself a wardrobe fit for a queen. A green wool dress with a herringbone pattern. A white cotton gown with blue trim and dimity. A ground silk handkerchief, no, three. Black crape shirt with gathering. A pair of leather shoes.

I miss, most, the shoe-binder. Of all the things to miss, his art. Take away the seamstress, the fine dressmaker, the straw-hat fashioner and the wood turner. I shall take the shoe-binder.

There is merriment aboard today. Surely we are not that close to the end of the voyage. The Surgeon is on desk speaking to the Captain, who sees all from the quarterdeck. The deck is being washed and we are instructed to clean with vinegar.

It smells like a shop back in London. Turn the corner and it entered the nose, that sting of vinegar, that heavy oily air. My stomach turns, not because of this but this, along with my monthly distress, it is almost too much. The padding Cord has given me is as stiff as an old loaf of bread. She says it's the salt in the water as does it. She says it's clean. But it hurts so, when walking or bending. And they think it is the vinegar that makes my eyes water so.

I watch for the glimpse of a fin. I know they are still out there somewhere. I am watching out instead of watching my own yard and so do not see the foot.

I'm down before I know it and someone is pressing on my chest, holding me so. I smell her before I see her. Cassie Jukes, like a massive rock formation above me. The one on my chest is a mindless player in this, and will do whatever she is told to do.

Cassie Jukes places her foot on my forehead. The shoe is broken, but the heel remains.

"Whoopsalie. I was jest walkin', ye see, and this piece of something as was stuck to me shoe, M'Lud, no notion when or 'ow it got there."

I am praying that not even Cassie Jukes is stupid enough to....

She spits and I feel it land on my face.

"Dontcha worry. You kin wait fer it, Lovie. I'm comin' for ye."

The release of pressure is more than I can bear.

Cord finds me gasping, sick, and takes me below. She wipes me off and checks my front for cracked bones.

"You'll be all colours soon," she tells me, helping me back into my dress. "I told you to stay away from her."

Chest and ribs are on fire, so I do not reply.

"You know what they do to tattlers down here," Cord mutters. "I've said as much as I dare to."

She helps me to bed and goes to inform the Surgeon that I have fallen.

And have I? Fallen?

The surgeon stops by and confirms the bruising, as it is already flaring. He assures me that my ribs are intact. He offers me something to help me sleep. I take it, but, as I am on watch, like the officers above, I do not drink it down.

I know the meaning of the word appeasement. I know it is a necessary word, like air. I have nothing at all. Caroline has only her shell, her shawl having gone while back in the prison. I tell Caroline, when she comes, that I am in need of some alcohol for my pain. She disappears and is gone a good long time. It is early evening when she returns and in the folds of her jacket is the flask.

"How?"

"He got it. Harkness. I told him it was for you and he got it."

She hands it to me. She actually thinks I mean to drink it.

"It's not for me." I pull it beneath the cover.

She looks puzzled.

I lie back and feel the rhythm of the ship. I am being rocked, Mother, do not worry on my account. I have my friend, you see, and she cares for me. Am I not fortunate? How things might have turned out! And here I am, Mother, quite alive.

Cassie Jukes is making her way to one of the mates. I hear that she makes good use of the 'tween deck. But another mate has taken a girl up on deck in the night. Caroline has spent some nights with Harkness. She could stay with him constantly. I do not know why she doesn't.

It is the following morning when the doctor says I am fit for work that I ask him if I may assist him. I will clean, wash, hold patients down, administer powders. He thinks, at first, that I am too young. I tell him I can read and he revises his opinion, saying that I may help with the women prisoners.

Thank you, Mother, for teaching me to read.

He tells me I must first wash and clean myself. While I do so he examines my bruises, lingering as he presses gently against my chest.

He tells me to dress, handing me a clean apron.

I am to administer to Izzy Watts, who remains in his care. I observe where he places his notebooks. I observe his store of powders and medicines.

Poor Izzy Watts. She has been roughly used by life. And now her poor mind is affected. When I return to the hold I tell Caroline of my new duties. She looks at me strangely.

"Don't worry," I tell her. "All is well."

She runs her hand along the beam, making little chopping motions.

"He wants me to stay with him," she says, and sounds so different now. The gruffness is gone from her voice, the young feral lad is gone. She sounds like a married sister, or an Auntie down on the boardwalk, buying ices for her niece.

"He wishes to marry you?"

She blushes. This is new.

"He must return shortly on another ship, so he will not have leave for some time. He would take me in, which might get me a Ticket of Leave."

Ticket of Leave? I am only now learning the distinctions that come our way upon arrival in the colony. I wish to speak more to her but Cassie Jukes approaches.

"Think you can hide from me up wit' surgeon? T'ain't time enough nor space on this ship for you te get way of me."

I think, now, that I hope this is true. For then there is no place for her to hide from me.

She scuttles away and I find the dead board, as I call it, which can be shifted. Here are my treasures; I have two. The cup of medicine that was supposed to make me sleep. And this flask of rum, a welcome addition.

I have a clean apron to wear at the surgeon's. I have Caroline, whose face is changed along with her voice.

The Good Book is brought to me this evening. The women are distracted. One is about to deliver her child and the agony is felt by all, it seems. I should, perhaps, read a healing psalm, but the book falls open to Malachi, and I read:

> *For, behold, the day cometh, that shall burn as an oven; and all the proud, yea, and all that do wickedly, shall be stubble: and the day that cometh shall burn them up....*

This offers them no immediate comfort, and I turn to Isaiah:

Remember ye not the former things, neither consider the things of old...
Behold, I will do a new thing; now it shall spring forth; shall ye not know it?
I will even make a way in the wilderness, and rivers in the desert...

�֎

Aris:	"Hey, how's it going?
Street guy:	—
Aris:	"Nice day, eh? Finally a decent day."
	[Loonie in cup.]
Street guy:	"Yeah. God bless you, Miss."

Does she fund this man in order to be called "Miss?" Is she condoning a fellow human being's existence under these conditions solely for the ego bump? Aris can't think straight this afternoon. The totally unnecessary meeting has her reeling. She hates pep talks, spirit squads, or whatever they're called. The boss's engagement to Treena notwithstanding, there seemed to be no reason to call a huddle half an hour before people were leaving for the weekend. Worse that she was expected to drop everything and go for a drink with 'the team', of which "Treener" was now a permanent member.

She is heading over to the archives later than she wanted to be. Friday night is a time she likes to keep open. Why? She can hear Dr. Grogan cheering her optimism.

Aris's grandmother would tell her that Friday nights were always entertainment evenings in the old days, and the entertainment was in the home. Her grandmother would fix an eye on young Aris and then murmur, "Piano. Singing. A little dancing if you fancied it. Everyone came prepared, you see. When it was your turn you had to perform. Everyone had something they did. Reciting, declaiming, singing, playing. I played and sometimes sang. It was good entertainment, not that rot as you see nowadays. And there was never anything done there as you wouldn't want your own mother to see."

Young Aris would nod, thinking of all the people who would come to her house when she was grown up. She would let somebody else play the piano. She hoped someone would tap dance.

Damn that Treena. She swooped in and ruined the entire dynamic of the place. *And* she threw out Aris's Tupperware.

Now Aris is late to the archives. Nobody is around on a Friday night. They're all at home slipping into their tap shoes. She sits at the terminal. The Reference Desk is closed, so she's on her own. The long windows betray little of the movement of trees and grass. They are Japanese prints, two-dimensional trees hovering above grasses and streams, flowers floating in air.

She calls up the ship's information once again. It arrives in New South Wales. Is this Sydney Harbour? It's definitely not Van Diemen's Land. Her map shows Hobart and Launceston. But there's also Newcastle…. What was it Dunstan said?

Parramatta.

What's it like to catch sight of land? Or, more likely, to be below and to hear the cheering as the men swing into action. And, on shore, are they crying out as well?

A ship! By God, a ship!

What happens to you, my girl? Aris muses.

Dunstan said she should go to the Australian sites now. Prison Registers. The Female Register.

"The *what*?"

"You'll want to read about Reverend Marsden," he said, before shooing her away as she dusted.

Samuel Marsden. Aris types the name in. Hit upon hit about a Reverend who provided…hit upon hit. "The Flogging Parson", chief Anglican in New South Wales. Hated Irish. Hated Catholics. Hated Irish Catholics above all. Hated women, too, it would seem, for his Female Register listed anyone not married as a concubine. And he wanted everyone married. By "married" he meant "Church of England" and by Church of England he meant married by him.

Aris knows there is more to it than this. Her brush with history in high school and university has taught her that cohabitation was simply that, a convenient match, or a love match, without the blessing of the church.

Given this Marsden, she's not sure that's such a bad thing. But to be labelled a concubine? What might Marsden have called Aris, a middle-aged spinster? Yes, that is exactly what he would have called her, as "spinster" was still used on some marriage forms in England. A young woman she knew married in her twenties and was listed on the form as "spinster." Aris would be a…what…fossil? She's well past her "best-before" date, as they say on Corrie. Or is it her "sell by" date? Either way, she has no suitor in the wings, a respectable widower with grown children who needs a fourth for bridge. No, she is a concubine to Marsden, albeit a superannuated one.

Lovely.

Strange how even from this time and distance she dislikes the zealot Reverend Marsden, his filthy-mouthed sermons against the Irish Catholics, his odious opinion of females.

She would not put Maura here. She reads that, upon arrival, the women prisoners are spruced up in whatever they have, and paraded before the men on shore. Officers, non-cons, and ex-cons. A marital cattle auction where the men pick and choose. If a married man takes her, she might be his wife's servant, or a servant as well as his mistress. If a single man takes her, she is his until he tires of her. So much for the Reverend's pure society.

Aris sits in the quiet room, quiet but loud in its silence. Air is moving and pushing past her ears. Whispers rise and speak to the high ceiling.

Maura Quell. Oh, Maura.

When Aris was a teenager she went to a couple of school dances, the first because she was naïve, the second because she hadn't learned from the first. Standing on the sidelines—they didn't even think to have little tables or chairs—watching the lights dim and the couples grope, she told herself that she was invisible. This was why nobody asked her to dance. But it was also why the evening wouldn't matter in the end. At least nobody had seen her there, alone, because *nobody saw her at all*. There were advantages to being invisible.

Could Maura do it?

Aris finds another site, Photographs of Convict Ships. Another. Harbour. Another. Prison.

Parramatta. The Female Factory.

Aris has taken a lot for granted, she really has. When she thinks of it, she's never actually needed a "protector." Sure, it was nice, better than nice, when Derek would pick her up after work, or take her out for dinner. It was pleasant to go home in a taxi with a slightly inebriated young man now and again. Or to know that the man two doors down would come to help if she had an emergency.

But to cower, hoping someone would take you in? Take you under their wing? In exchange for you being taken into their bed? To be called every name for simply being what you are, single and female?

No, Reverend Marsden. We would not get along. You would not share my salad. I would not give up my seat on the bus for you.

But it is different for her girl, isn't it?

It is strange the way Aris's mind works. She's aware of the absurdity of it, but she finds herself strangely pleased that, in her mind at least, Maura hasn't arrived yet. She's still on board ship. She is still safe.

I have been caring for Izzy Watts but there is little that will help her. Her pain is inside, and she has found her own way.

Surgeon Matthews allows me to sit with her, to wipe her forehead. Days pass. Sometimes it is scrubbing aprons and bandages, soaking linens, removing foul buckets, and the like. I am calm as a dove.

Medicines are little powders. Packets. Vials. He is so clever. He shows me a book with the human form, all in pieces. I have never before thought this way, yet I know. I have seen soldiers with parts of their shadows missing in the sun of late afternoon. I am aware. And yet I never thought of a person so made up, so structured.

"It's a terrible marvel, is it not?" I say to him and he looks up from his notes.

"Yes. Yes, it is. Terrible and marvellous, both."

It is after this that he leaves me for short times. A mate by the name of Weston is in the berth with a deep gash in his foot. The wound is clean but the surgeon worries about infection, so we watch and change bandages.

"Does it hurt horribly?"

I am imagining our Lord on the Cross, His pain worse than all of ours, but this old tar, Weston, smiles up at me and shakes his head.

"Not much. These feet are like leather."

Still, I see him move his leg with care. He sleeps now, along with Izzy. I have washed around the table, the desk. Surgeon Matthews is still missing. I finger his notebooks, wander to the not yet replaced and locked away vials. I am not sure what this one is for, but it smells strong and stings my nose. Shall he miss it? I cannot take the entire contents so I pour a portion into a tiny bottle and stopper it. It slips into my apron pocket like a slender finger into a glove.

I return below deck and find the dead board and add it to my growing treasure trove.

Caroline holds my hand in the night. She sleeps fitfully. I am on watch for Cassie Jukes. She has been persecuting another one, this time an Irish. She uses her cruellest tongue on them, and she has taken most of the woman's garments so the Irish must roam the deck barely decent. I have nothing to offer her, or I would. It is not possible to take an apron from the surgeon. Cord cannot help, for she has nothing either.

"That one's got a throne waiting for her in the flames," is all she will say, nodding to Cassie Jukes.

It is Caroline who does it. She who also has nothing has somehow provided a parchment-thin garment a fairy princess might wear underwater, for the shift fairly floats in the air. That said, it is sure to be a comfort to the woman, who is thanking Caroline and making the Sign of the Cross, blessing my friend, her children, and her relations for all eternity.

Just as the Irish turns to put it on, the odorous one returns.

The Irish shrieks and runs, her breasts shifting and bobbing. Cassie Jukes yells an obscenity that will reach down to hell itself, then glares at Caroline. I have never seen her this inflamed; if fire could come from the eyes, both Caroline and I would be burned to cinders.

"You've done it!" she snarls. "Say yer prayers." She points a claw in our faces.

Tonight.

I have not chosen the time or place. I have not, Mother, made up the conditions.

Caroline is uneasy all day. Harkness speaks with her on deck. He is of another order of beings, far removed from our squabbles below deck. I am hoping he will take her to him this evening, as I have things to do.

Caroline comes to me as we eat our meal. She is resolute. Whether she still has fears, I do not know. But we are two fierce gargoyles in a church tower, strong in our resolve, cool to the touch.

Marsh has handed me a round green stone on a chain. Where has this some from? What is a young man like him doing with such a fine, thin chain? The green stone—I know not what it is for I've never seen such as stone, nor such a colour—is beyond belief and beauty. Midshipman Harkness had only a shell on a string.

"Want to put it on?" he asks.

This is closer than he has ever stood.

"Here, it goes like this."

And his arms about me as the chain falls round my neck.

"It was my mother's," he says.

"No one has ever given me such a thing as this."

Saying a mere thank you is not enough. What am I to say?

I take his calloused hand and squeeze it. The roughness reminds me of my mother's hand when she'd sing a little song, her hand brushing across my forehead.

Marsh's clear eyes glint.

And I have a fourth treasure.

I do not know how Cassie Jukes manages it, but she bribes the guards and prisoners alike. She knows the watch above deck this night, when and how often they pass.

I know she will not come alone, but she will not bring a crowd, not for what she wishes to do. As expected, she comes with only one, the sad Irish that accepted the shift from Caroline. I believe she means Caroline and me to be a warning to the woman.

We approach.

"Ye arrogant tripe, foolish enough, I'll grant ye that."

Caroline puts herself, yet again, between Cassie and me.

"I'm the one as gave her the shift. It's me you want."

"Aaaawww, innit pretty? Lovie, 'ere, and 'er bedmate, like a proper couple o'...."

"I've some to apologize," I say, pushing past Caroline.

Caroline starts. The Irish watches.

"That's right. I've come to offer you restitution…gifts."

"You what?"

She does not trust it.

"Don't believe me? Pity. Because I've brought you all sorts."

And I open my bindle cloth of treasures. The flask Caroline procured, the necklace from Marsh.

"See? How about a drink?"

Cassie Jukes fondles the necklace.

"Put me." She commands the Irish, the marvellous stone lost in her filthy garments.

"Unstopper the flask."

I am only too happy to oblige, as Caroline watches, unbelieving.

Cassie Jukes yanks the bottle from my hand and takes a swallow. And another.

I feel myself tingling as if it were me drinking, not her.

"Maura…the necklace…Marsh," Caroline says, her eyes confused.

"Oy, where'd you get this?"

I am about to say, when Caroline owns to this as well.

"Well, it tastes funny."

"Oh, come on. I've never seen you pass up a drink, now, have I? What's wrong with it? Not suitable?" I mock her. "Not to M'Lady's standards of backstreet gin?"

She continues pouring it in, of course, even as she complains. She barks to the Irish to settle her on her backside.

"Ye…bloody wretches, always tryin'…te get around…ye whinnying little mares wot got yer 'eads…oy…I feel bad. This is foul, this is…wotcha done te…."

She is starting to swim now, faster than I expected.

"Getcha 'ere," she is trying to motion to the Irish but her hand is wavering. She manages to pull her blade, a longer one than that which I threw overboard, and the moon on the blade casts a spell, like a fish in water, flashing. She reaches her arm back to plunge and falls forward with the wayward strike, crumpling in on herself.

Caroline, who has said nothing, now stands beside me. All three of us are there. I do not know about the Irish.

"Here," Caroline commands, pulling the twisted cord from around her neck. I watch as the Irish ties Cassie Jukes' hands, the shell still attached to the cord. Caroline stuffs the bindle rag into Cassie Jukes' mouth.

She is heavy, so heavy as I lift. She is horrible and heavy and I don't know what I should have done without them there to help. Silent and with good speed we are starboard, aft. We are praying for a shooting star or something to distract.

"Wait," I whisper, grappling with the mound. I feel it, the chain, and rip it from her neck.

"Right," I say, and we pray as one as we angle the foul dung heap over the side.

The ship plies the water. The wake moves outward like arms embracing the sea. We stand, shivering, in the moonlight. And I am standing in Fish Street, again, calling for Eugene. I am grinding my fists into my stomach to ease the hurt and the bitter crunching of my fears.

Eugene!

His long lashes against my arm as he sleeps.

Sleep well now, Eugene. Cover yourself. Sleep.

"Now what?" trembles the Irish.

Now the sharks that I pray have followed the ship will be rewarded for their fortitude.

"Maura!"

Caroline.

"Each of us goes back down," Caroline says. "Not a word. You first," she says to the Irish. Caroline grasps the woman's arm. "What do you know of this evening?"

The woman puts her other hand atop Caroline's.

"God bless you, Miss. I know nothing at all."

She is off, leaving Caroline and me alone. I expect her to ask it, so I answer.

"We've done what we had to. We've done what's right."

Caroline puts her arms round me and presses her forehead into mine.

"We've done what we had to. We've not done what's right."

She kisses me then and I know we have sealed our souls. Our bargain with the world is complete. The green stone in my hand is cool and steady. We slip down below deck into our prison.

Of course she is missed. The foul as well as the fair are missed in this life, although only the fair are mourned.

We are lined up on deck. Cord has a distinctly happy look about her face, as have many other women. The Irish is a statue, a silent one. The captain informs us that, following a search, it has been determined that we have lost a prisoner overboard. He is enraged, or confounded, or both, as to how this can have occurred. There will be recriminations among his officers, and this fills me with worry lest something should happen to Harkness. The Captain wishes to converse with Cord and other women who speak for the prisoners.

Midshipman Harkness addresses us.

"Does anyone have knowledge or information as to what happened to…."

Here he checks his list.

"…Cassie Jukes? You know her, I assume?"

Groaning, grunting, a yelp.

"People do not disappear," Harkness says, panning across the lot of us.

"The Captain has ordered that all of you are confined below deck until further notice."

We file down. The lanterns flicker as we assemble round the table, a crowd of scarecrows.

"So," Cord says, "something happened to Cassie Jukes."

A lusty cheer goes up. It is wrong but wholehearted.

"Wouldn't think you could lose something that big," she continues.

"Or that stinking," someone adds.

"So."

"So."

It is the strangest speech I have ever heard.

"We'll be down here for a while," Cord says. "But I, for one, have found it much more bearable of late."

Nods from the mob.

"Let's not become animals, ourselves. We'll divide her spoils in an orderly fashion. I propose that people claim what they lost to her first."

Cord goes about organizing a station down by Cassie Jukes' corner.

It is so simple. I sit with Caroline. She has found a tiny length of string and is trying to repair the broken chain of my necklace.

"I'm sorry about your shell," I say, as she puts the chain back round my neck.

She is with me tonight. Both of us should be able to sleep well. No one must keep watch anymore. And yet we don't sleep. I believe she wishes to be with Harkness, but the hatch is firmly locked.

I do not know why I cannot sleep. My mind wanders off in all directions. I am only bodily on this ship. This realization is new.

That I am only bodily here. That my mind can take me anywhere. That I can be home with you, Mother, with Eugene. That I can go to the forest or the cathedral.

No. Not the cathedral. Not now.

Mother. Please don't turn away. I know. I know.

My tears mark trails down my face and burn my ears. I look over and Caroline's face is like a death mask, but, I think, she sleeps.

✼

Gas prices fluctuate up, so every man jack of the populace is taking the bus. Aris should be happy. The little eco-warrior in her should be cheering. But she sees it on all the faces of the regulars. The Seat Saver has suddenly squeezed his knees together, buttocks holding as he rides. The woman reading tomes has switched to newspapers, her eye flitting up for a wayward knapsack or a face full of briefcase. The bus drivers, too, are feeling it, asking people to move to the rear, to stay clear of the doors.

Aris is wedged between a woman with gagging cologne—doesn't she read the signs?—and a distinctly disaffected young man. His t-shirt sports a drawing of a smiling doll-like face with stitches all over it. An eye is loose in its socket. He probably does intake work at the hospital, your first contact with the medical system.

"You sick?"

Patient nods.

"Sick! Fill out these forms."

Hasn't she heard the kids saying that, "sick" as if it is something good? No different than when people used to say "bad."

"You one bad Mama."

Well, not Aris.

But "sick" as good is something the stubborn grammarian in her refuses to acknowledge.

Big day. Treener is leaving for her pre-wedding preps. Dunstan should be back at work. Aris finds herself humming through a debate on aggressive drug therapy, and her smaller, more fridge-friendly Tupperware container is still where she left it that morning.

Today has potential.

"Great that they'll be gone four weeks, eh?" Aris says to new co-op student, Dave.

"Oh...yeah."

"Where I come from that's a month." Aris says.

"Yeah. Sick," he replies.

Dunstan is, in fact, on duty when Aris arrives. His workday will be ending shortly but she sees him waiting by her terminal—she privately refers to it as such—and he smiles when she approaches.

"Hey, good to see you back," Aris smiles, feeling her face stretch in an unaccustomed direction.

"Good to see my back? Are you trying to get rid of me?" he smiles. His bachelor trousers look professionally pressed.

"You look...nice. Like...."

"Like what?"

"You look ready...."

"Ready to take on the world? Not quite."

He is still moving carefully, but he has lost a few pounds and he cuts a dashing moon-faced figure as he steps to the photocopier.

"Oh...here...."

He passes her a small sheet of yellow paper. On it is a simple drawing of a bouquet of flowers.

"Uh...nice."

"They're in the staff room. To say thank you for your concern. For...."

He is struggling.

"...for your friendship. It made the time pass."

Aris stares at the screen. Is she blinking?

"That's what I do best. Make the time pass."

It is a good thing that their lives do not depend on their witty repartee. Aris is aware of Dunstan Regimbald's wool vest as he stands beside her clicking her keys.

"Here. This site. She might be here. Or...well, there are lists, Tickets of Leave, Pardons, and stuff like that. But first it would be good to find our girl."

Aris pores over lists and documents. Dunstan speaks to a woman about military men of the Expeditionary Force. He seems glad to be back. Aris sees how he deals with each person as if the questions posed are new to him, as if their relations were the most important people in the world. They're probably shoemakers, mariners, farmers.

Aris spends an hour or so working. She hasn't looked up from the screen once and when she does she sees that the Reference Desk is closed. He left without saying good night?

Aris hasn't found a thing. What does it mean? Maura was on the bloody boat. Where is she?

It is dark grey outside. The bus shelter has a new billboard up, importuning her to shop at the downtown mall. A woman with watermelon-flesh-coloured lips is calling to her. The woman's teeth are blinding.

Where is Dunstan? Where are her bloody flowers?

Oh yes, Dr. Grogan, she knows it's all in the attitude. Just like she should smile benignly skateboarding athlete who has barely missed her foot.

Cats overhead. Now she knows why cats have always creeped her out. They don't *mind* crawling around in her head. Aris runs a bath. Cats hate water, don't they? She puts some Bebel Gilberto on and tries to get a kink out of her neck. She aches. Nice. She's middle-aged and she aches. The bath is perfect, though, forgiving all the day's trials.

As she is lying there breathing in pomegranate and citrus, she thinks of Maura Quell. Aris would make a hopeless prisoner. She can't imagine a world where complaining would have no standing. Sure, she has cats in her brain and idiots in the city, but to be a prisoner? With no rights? No recourse?

Aris sinks lower into the warm suds.

The ringing telephone is cruel. How often does that thing ring? Aris wraps the generous, thirsty towel around herself and bounds into the living room. Is she mistaken or have the cats stopped scampering overhead?

"Hello," Aris mutters, as she stubs her toe on the coffee table leg.

"Uh...hello."

A tentative stalker. Great.

"Hello, what do you want?"

"Want? Uh, well, it's Dunstan."

Aris starts, suddenly quite naked, a sensation that was absent when she thought this was a telemarketer from Delhi or a sensitive kidnapper.

"Dunstan! Hi. How'd...you get my number?"

He chuckles. "It's like mine. Not too many A. Sandalls in the book."

Asshole Sandall. Candy Ass.

"No." She is starting to get cold.

"Say, Dunstan...."

"I wanted to apologize for cutting out."

"What? Nonsense. No, you were finished work and...."

"Your flowers. But I had to leave suddenly. Sorry. Still some post-operative fine-tuning. I...I had to leave right away. I'm sorry."

"Are you okay? Is everything okay?"

He shrugs. She can feel him shrug.

"Yeah. I'm not 100% yet, let's just put it that way."

"I didn't find anything. No ship's muster; no name on a list. Then I got this bad feeling. Remember when it listed that there were one hundred and twenty-two passengers that began the journey but only one hundred and twenty-one that arrived? You don't think...."

Dunstan's voice is reassuring.

"No. Listen. She's young. She's a London girl by the time she leaves. Our girl is tough."

They sit there for a while discussing Maura Quell. The next step will be to try and find the Convict Indent, Dunstan says.

They talk about cats, other peoples' cats. They talk about how nice Aris's flowers are, blooming in the staff room at the archives. They laugh at the idea of Bruce, the technician, employing the bouquet in his effort to get laid.

"It's not *that* nice a bouquet," Dunstan says.

It is only when she feels quite frozen that she tells him she must go. She could reveal that she was in the bathtub when he called, but then it would sit there between them on the phone line, demanding to be addressed.

She thanks him for his call and hangs up.

The cats have definitely stopped roaming. They are piled in a lump atop the body of Aris's neighbour, feasting away contentedly.

Aris.

Dr. Grogan, the avatar, appears to chastise. But what is this? Is he pleased, or perhaps even a little smug?

Yes, Dr. Grogan. I had a naked phone call. Does this count as phone sex?

She can see him, eyebrow rising as he adds the information to his Glowing Portrait of Patient Aris Sandall.

Candy Ass.

Tonight she turns off Jimmy Fallon and the talk show boys and lies in the dark. She imagines her bed a small boat, and she is so relaxed, so comfortable there, on her back, that she lets it take her wherever it will, the ocean wide, all horizons possible.

We are locked in more often than not now, as we near our destination. The water has been rough of late. Surgeon Matthews has examined me a great deal, and with much interest. His hands do what they do, or what they must, as mine have done. I am no one to judge.

Caroline Lockett has been with Midshipman Harkness. She has hardly come down at night. Her space is empty, and someone has taken her ragged cloth of a blanket. Midshipman Harkness has given her another shell. I have seen it round her neck.

The green stone of Marsh is heavy on my throat. He wishes me to go with him. He wants to speak with me but I have not felt like speaking with anyone, especially not a young man with an open face and an easy countenance, though one evening I dreamed of his sandy-coloured hair and saw my hand moving through it.

The women wanted me to read from the Book. I began but the words could not get out and I choked. It was Hettie Rags Crenshaw who told them to leave me alone. She has come back a little since the departure of Cassie Jukes. She does not strut as she once did, but nor does she stoop.

"Awww, leave 'er be. Can't ye see she's ill?" she said, and they let me be. I looked at her then and, just for a moment, our eyes met. That this fellow feeling occurred was terrible, terrible but real nonetheless.

I have been dreaming of Eugene as well. O, Mother, I pray he did not believe I had abandoned him.

Abandonment is, I think, the worst of all. Didn't Our Lord cry out on the Cross, "Why hast Thou forsaken me?"

I did not abandon him, Mother. I promise you that.

Yet I expect nothing. Certainly not forgiveness.

I am now what I am, what I have come to be.

Surgeon Matthews says he may be able to apply for a Ticket of Leave for me, which only the Governor can grant. I do not believe his words, said as he fumbles with himself. I will go with the lot of them, those that are not chosen.

Caroline wishes, I believe, to remain with Midshipman Harkness. But this may prove difficult as his service will come first. Perhaps he will one day marry her, and my History of Caroline Lockett will come to pass. Caroline by the hearth, rocking a cradle, tending a garden. Her dress will be whole and trimmed with tatted lace, her hair plaited and her hands clean. Unlike mine.

She comes to me as I scrub the surgery. She is an older sister now, or feels like one, holding my shoulders and speaking as an older sister speaks. She asks me about Surgeon Matthews, and about Marsh.

I see Marsh's smile when I dim the shades of my eyes. He is in full sun, his own eyes mere slits in his laughing face.

I feel Surgeon Matthews' bulk as his hands examine me.

"Matthews has a wife," Caroline says.

I see the strong legs of Marsh as he climbs the rigging.

And, always, I see the lolling head of Cassie Jukes, a rag warping her mouth into an "O"; I see her dropping off the ship like a crumb from the dinner table.

Cord says to mind myself and to consider my situation. She says I should take what is offered.

"Look at me," she says. "I know where I'll end up."

I miss Caroline. I reach across for her hand in the night, but the berth is empty.

Marsh enters the surgery, though he has no cause to do so. He struggles, as I do, to speak. He believes me to be a "good sort" and he would be proud to be with me. He knows we've all been transported for "trinkets and trifles." He would not hold it against me, he says.

"You have spirit, Maura Quell."

His honest eyes torture me.

"Someone will have you!" He pleads.

Why not he? Why not someone it is easy to look upon, someone whose age and demeanor is not so different from my own?

"They're old men, there. Old for you, girl. Do you want that?"

He smells of male sweat and salt air. I reach for his hair and, just once, see my hand as it is in my dream, caught in his sand-coloured hair.

It is bitterness of the soul that prevents me. What I have become prevents me, shuts away the other history I was making up for myself, shuts it away and opens only one path.

He is crestfallen. He cannot look at me. Even less so when I return to him the lovely green stone on the chain, which will some day grace the throat of his betrothed, his mother's or his grandmother's prize on the winner of Marsh's heart. The stone, cool as always, passes from my hand. I shall remember it around my neck. But I also remember it around the neck of Cassie Jukes. So lies my fate; so lies the sanction on my heart.

The ship is being cleaned and readied. The surgery is empty but for Izzy Watts, whom Surgeon Matthews tells me will go directly to a prison.

Her body is young but it is weak and unhealthy. Her skin is pallid and her teeth rot in her head. I do not think she will be long for this world. It is when I am washing her chest that I see, embroidered inside the bodice of her dress, a Cross, a flower, perhaps a tulip, and these words: "Love to Isabel."

I comb her hair. Love to Isabel. I clean beneath her nails and wash her feet. Love to Isabel.

"She's gone," I whisper as I adjust her blanket. "You're free."

And spend the rest of the day pondering what I meant by telling a prisoner like Izzy Watts that she was free.

I stand on the deck and take in the horizon. It has been my companion. I realize with a start that it has always been there, always leading me toward it.

Just because I am alone does not mean I have nowhere to go.

The Convict Indent. Dunstan says she would surely have had one, as it was the official document of her arrival in the colony.

"What, like an immigration document?" Aris asks, poking her fish filet.

"It was the main form. It was, like, an identity paper. Everything was supposed to be recorded on it as you went along: the trial, the sentencing, the trip over and anything of interest that happened to you in the colony. Of course...."

He pauses to smell his bread roll.

"...the earlier forms didn't have as much information."

"Of course," Aris repeats.

"I've...been meaning to ask you something," Dunstan says. Bruce walks by in time to hear this and acknowledges Dunstan with a wink worthy of a Monty Python moment. Dunstan has revealed that Bruce now resides, part-time, in *Second Life*, where his love life is going much better than it is here on earth. What is Bruce implying by his gesture? What has Dunstan said to him about her?

"You...you haven't actually gone about trying to determine whether our...Maura...is in fact your relative. I mean, most people come at genealogy "front-to-back." In fact, it's recommended. You, on the other hand, have jumped backward without a net."

"Without a net?"

"Without the branches, then. You know, that hold the tree together."

Aris's red pepper is technicolour, like the faces were on her grandmother's brand new colour TV when Aris was a child. Beet red people fell in love with lime green people, and they drove away in grape coloured cars.

"Don't you want to know, you know, if she's actually related?"

Aris realizes she has been dreading this moment. He is right. People do this genealogy thing to find out who they come from, to shake out the skeletons or to gloat over musty old princes. And her? Who is this girl to her?

"You said yourself that she was just a name your grandmother used to keep you in line. Maybe she was someone the family knew, back then. Or maybe it was a random name…."

"Oh, yeah. A typical name? Maura Quell?"

"Well, I don't know, Aris Sandall. Speaking as Dunstan Regimbald, I can only say…."

"Look, why are you doing this? Now?"

Irritation? Or is it fear?

"I don't know. Maybe…maybe because she's so important to you. To us. Part of me wants to know, for your sake."

"And the other part's afraid, right? Afraid she's a name in a book? Or on a Convict Indent? Well, that's how I feel."

They sit in silence as Bruce glances over, trying to catch Dunstan's attention. No doubt he thinks that Dunstan has been rebuffed. He has been trying to get Dunstan interested in *Second Life* and online dating for a while now.

Back to work. The trees are cheering her on outside the window, waving and twirling little rally rags. Or maybe it's just a plastic bag. Dunstan is back behind the desk, where he is assisting an elderly man with a list of questions.

Aris accesses Convict Lists and tries for the Convict Indents.

New South Wales.

Sydney.

Come on.

Dunstan whisks by with the gentleman and drops her a note. What, is she in grade five? It feels like it, palming the scrap of paper. There's a web-site listed. Underneath he's scribbled, *Looked up Winchell, the part about the puppets. Artificial hearts. Wooden faces smiling. Building a fake heart for a real person to use.* He's signed it with an "X."

Aris hasn't felt a flush like this since peri-menopause began. Back to work. She plugs in the web-site.

Convict Indents!

She reads through the first few. The handwriting is elaborate, ornate even. Aris imagines someone sitting at an outpost desk, picking up a pen and dipping it in the ink, making a few sweeping motions with his arms before setting pen to paper.

Martin Kritch, he writes.
Martin Kritch, per ship, the "Screw-Up" arrived 4 May 1808, was tried at London Assizes 14 August 1807. Sentence fourteen years for being a fuck-up back home. Worked ass off in Colony, granted a Ticket of Leave….

Even there. Even then. Bureaucracy.

She wishes history was better organized. If people would just stay put long enough so one could record their name, rank and serial number; if they would just lie down and die in neat little rows in numbered graves, or in their proper beds at night, in their proper embraces.

Oh, Maura, girl, where are you?

The Female Register. What about that? What about this Marsden?

The artificial heart is not a solution, It is meant to ensure blood flow while the human heart is inactive. No artificial means has yet been deemed superior to the fully-functional human heart; however, research indicates potential….

Her own life has gaps like this. The early years following her parents' accident. The first year after she and Derek split
She simply disappeared—from the map, from the record. She slipped

out while they were sharpening pencils and dipping nibs, while they were lining up people and checking their teeth.

If she can do this so effectively in her own time, what chance, what hope, is there of finding Maura Quell? Yet it is important to know that she is Aris's own, Aris's family, her own blood. It is so important that she cannot possibly take the chance….

Dr. Grogan, you are right. A glass half-full.

She can hear the wags debating why, if one is going for broke, why the glass can't be completely full? And she wants to scream back at them, because then there's the possibility that it might be completely empty! So she'll wrap her hand around the tumbler, thank you, and keep watch over its contents, knowing the vagaries of spillage, the physics of evaporation.

Dunstan has offered to meet her after work; rather, to stay on until she arrives. He has material that he wants her to see. That, and a completely unnecessary but sweet replacement bouquet of flowers.

"Bruce doesn't need these in *Second Life*," Dunstan said when he called.

They joke about Bruce but the funny thing is that Bruce seems a lot happier since joining his new life. Dunstan says he's easier to work with, and he even dresses better, although this would hardly seem to matter.

This has been puzzling Aris. How can what amounts to an imaginary life make such changes in his real one? Doesn't he know it's false? Doesn't he know that he's still Bruce the library technician, late of the Triple XXX Adult Superstore, whose physical activity is limited to a weekly dip in the hockey pool?

Yet, when she gets to the archives and Bruce is checking out, doesn't he smile—smile!—and wave an ink-stained hand her way?

"Saw Bruce downstairs," Aris tells Dunstan.

"Yeah. He left a bit early. Big date tonight, I think."

"What, a…?"

"*Second Life*. It's getting serious."

She is about to sit at her terminal when Dunstan leads her over to one of the long, polished tables.

"Here," he says.

She sits and looks up at him.

"Okay. Don't get mad at me. I couldn't help looking. I spent most of last night...I...found something."

Aris's pulse jumps.

"I know you wanted to...."

"Never mind that. What is it?"

He produces a sheet of paper.

"The Convict Indent," he breathes.

Aris stares. It is in the ornate handwriting she now identifies with all period documents. She picks up the form; the trees outside whisper.

Police History of Maura Quell
Maura Quell per ship "Canada" (2) arrived 8 September 1810 was tried at London Assizes 20 September 1809 Sentence Seven Years.
Parramatta Female Factory.
Merriweather Household
Parramatta Female Factory?

"This is an incomplete record," Dunstan says the obvious. He is always saying the obvious.

"So she went to the Female Factory," Aris says, stating the obvious herself.

"Yes, but, you see, they usually record what happened after that. Lots of people went into private service, or they married. They got on with their lives."

"But this is so unsure. She went back to the prison? To jail? And where is her pardon? When does she go free?"

Dunstan puts his hand atop hers.

"There's still the Female Register, if we can find her. There are still a few possibilities. Lots of the forms were lost or waylaid. It's not clear this one wasn't left uncompleted."

Glass half-full.

Aris sits with Dunstan, an archives employee and a client, hand in hand. The setting sun outlines the trees from behind, throwing them into relief. She knows the buses are out there, noisy, full, spewing chemicals into the air. She knows the trees are working against it, even as they sway and dance. Dunstan's slightly sweaty hand is calm and real in her own. Together, they walk over to the terminal.

So it begins. Rousted and told to wash up as best we are able. Some are not capable and I know I will be called to assist as I have been working with Surgeon Matthews. We are given vats of sea water to wash ourselves and our clothes in. When the garments dry they will be salt-stiff on us, like the sails.

I wash Caroline's hair, remembering the first time I saw her, the dark shadow around her head. Her hair is longer, and longer still when wet, and I hold her head in my hands and want to weep. What will happen to us now?

Cord says we must make ready for what is to come. She talks to me about choosing one man to protect me, and how it is better to go with one of them than to be left open to many. If she knew what Surgeon Matthews had said she would tell me to go with him.

His hair is thin and he has large ears, and his eyebrows are fierce. He pressed up against me in the surgery, wrapped his hands about my waist from behind and whispered in my ear that I could serve him, but I pulled away. He scowled, then, and said that I would become the natural of a settler in the colony, some rough brute who would beat me and share me as if I were a spittoon or a saddle. He said that, then banned me from the surgery. As I tried to push past him he reached for me and made me hold him…place my hand…he forced this upon me and I could not move past it. It was there and I watched his face as he grimaced and groaned.

I fled as he sat, eyes closed, open to the world. I fled to my prison, thinking how, if the Almighty took him, then and there, how he would arrive before the throne of God.

Cord asks me to help with Hettie Crenshaw. There is no cleaning her up, old mort. She is an ancient piece of mutton, ragged and pickled. Her hair crawls, rearranging itself in curious patterns atop her head. I replace her broken hat atop the mess, its veil a wisp of spiderwebs. Her legs are spindles, and are bitten and bruised. I try to sit her in a vat to scrub the worst off, but she will have none of it, like an old alley cat that would prefer to lick its wounds after a fight.

And who can blame her? She is going to be locked away. She has no future any longer on land. Better to cast her adrift here and now, provision a boat with a crust and a jug, than to take her ashore. She would not even be food for sharks.

She pulls her torn shirt close around her and gives me a glance that I once would have feared.

"All right, then, you," I say, far more gently than I expected to. I take her arm and help her away from the water.

"Can't make me more beautiful than what I am," she mutters, revealing the only remnant of Hettie Rags Crenshaw.

Caroline has a ribbon in her hair. He must have given it to her. I am about to say something when she reaches in her pocket and retrieves another, just like hers, a piece of hers.

"Harkness," she says. "Wear it. It will bring you luck."

But what is luck? And luck in what form? Caroline is expecting a servant position. She is hoping Harkness will return to her. She hopes we may find positions close to one another.

"I saw Marsh earlier," she says, looking past my indifferent face. "Are you sure about him?" she asks, reaching for and holding my hand. "He seems a good enough man."

O, Caroline. He visits my dreams often enough. His strong legs appear as I think of him and I must stare, instead, at the slop bucket to bring myself back.

"No. I can't."

I do not know if I should tell her about Surgeon Matthews. I decide to remain silent. It is at this moment that I know how it easy it is to become a stone, how Caroline's mysterious silence in the beginning was, perhaps, just a decision made on a Tuesday evening when the hands stopped turning on the grandfather clock and the birds were asleep in the branches.

Silence.

Simpler than these many stories.

"Land, ho!" someone bellows.

Marsh? They are all yelling, running, shouting. The ship creaks and seems to lurch forward, or maybe that is all of us leaning, with our hearts, in the direction of land.

Cord feels it is time for a prayer, or a reading from the Book. She cannot understand why I will not comply.

"You must," she proffers, but I cannot.

It is Caroline who takes it then, Caroline the mute, the fool, the natural of Midshipman Harkness. She turns to a passage. She is reading, she says, from Jeremiah.

> *Behold, I will bring them from the north country, and gather them from the coasts of the earth, and with them the blind and the lame, the woman with child and her that travaileth with child together: a great company shall return thither. They shall come with weeping, and with supplications will I lead them: I will cause them to walk by the rivers of waters in a straight way, wherein they shall not stumble: for I am a father to Israel, and Ephraim is my firstborn.*

She stops and stares at their rapt faces. She closes the book, hands it back to Cord, and shuffles to the side.

"So, are we ready then?" Cord asks. Does she expect anyone to reply? Look at them. O Lord, have mercy on this lot.

We are up on deck. I squint to see the headlands but cannot. But I am dizzy from the smell. Can they not all sense it? Land. The green air, everywhere, and such perfumes as I never knew in London. Strange birds I do not know streak overhead, and the choppy water dances. My eyes sting even though Caroline holds my hand. I would stay with her. I would go anywhere with her. I know this now.

Marsh's eyes meet mine, and I hope to smile at him but can only manage a painful grimace. His eyes I will remember. His smile. His sandy hair.

This charged air, vegetation, birds. Someone asks how long it has been since we left England. Captain speaks to an officer who conveys it to a mate. The scrawny throat stretches and yells, "It's an 'undred and sixty-nine days!"

One hundred and sixty-nine days.

Time for a babe to be born and die on board, for poor Izzy Watts to misplace her senses. Time for Cassie Jukes to fall in a drunken stupor overboard after a night rife with vices.

Time for Caroline to regain her voice.

For Maura Quell to damn herself for all eternity.

O, Mother, I arrive a felon of the crown, embracing my penance, as I embraced my decision. The girl who would go with Caroline to serve in a settler's house and earn her way back into favour is the same girl who caught her fingers in the string twisted round the hands of Cassie Jukes, the string with the shell, who felt her footing lift, and who plummeted over the side, as surely as Cassie Jukes fell, into the shark deep waters. She is another missing prisoner, even as we prepare to line up for inspection. Caroline stands behind me, her hands, briefly, on my shoulders, to steady me.

I am remembering, Mother, the part from Lamentations. What is it?

He hath set me in dark places, as they that be dead of old.
He hath hedged me about, that I cannot get out: he hath
made my chain heavy.
Also when I cry and shout, he shutteth out my prayer.

I have been read well and true. I have been read utterly.
And thou hast removed my soul far off from peace....

Mother, is there something, then, in this affliction and homelessness? Is there a home this far away?

For I must be where I am. We have arrived.

�֎

143

It says that she went to a household. Which would mean she got out of the horrible jail. Aris has been reading about it, essentially slave labour, girls doing needlework, washing clothes, making hats, carding wool. No relief from the overseers. No relief from one another.

She would have been bothered. There were men there. She was just a girl. She would have been bothered….

Aris finds she can't bring herself to say it, to voice any of her twenty-first century concerns. She can't spout the obvious with her customary "of course" added for effect.

Maura was a young girl, alone. She had to make her way from the ship, where God knows what had happened to her, to the jail. The jail, Aris knows, was primitive. Violence. Filth.

Aris thinks of her scented oils.

Dunstan had stayed with her while she searched for the Female Register. No luck. At around 8:30 she realized that he must be tired, having been there since the morning.

"You should go," she'd said. "Really. You're still recovering. I'm not going to find anything tonight."

Which sounded like someone waving off a fishing buddy. *Take off, eh? They're not biting.*

It was odd to think of them all there, swimming in the past, watching the lines fall across the water. Should they take the bait? Aris remembered fly fishing with a friend's uncle one summer, the spring in the long pole she flicked backward and then across the water. She remembered the momentum, how it shifted somewhere overhead, behind her, from something she was controlling to something that had a will of its own, the falling forward into water inevitable.

Plunk.

Their eyes watching from below.

Another one. She is not going home.

Dr. Grogan would have something to say about the way she is bonding with this speck, this drowsy fish in the stream. He might question his first advice, and wish that she had taken up scrapbooking. He would note that Aris's maternal instincts have raced forward into the breach. And he would take the mangled metaphor further and then would wind up making breach-blocks for machine guns at some fish plant.

Dr. Grogan would see right through her. You sad, middle-aged so and so, he'd say—or would, if his job didn't depend on it—you and Derek should have had a child. That way, it would be your teenager you were worrying over instead of some forgotten name in a roster. Dr. Grogan is married, isn't he? Successful wife, a kid or two up on blocks in the driveway. Yes, poor Aris. Poor coldstream Aris.

All the way home on the bus she listens to a couple argue about their kitchen cabinets. Molding. Some home reno crap, the new religion.

> She: You don't see it, do you? It doesn't work with the backsplash.
> He: I liked the one piece thing.
> She: Your eye follows it. It's all wrong.
> Aris: Your days are reeling out. Forget the fucking backsplash.

She should be sleeping. She should be resting so she can tackle the convention proceedings in the morning. Aris opens her closet. In this old apartment, the closet was the one unaccountable perk, abnormally large for the small room.

She takes out one hanger, then another. Clothes pile on the bed, costumes, uniforms. Here is her librarian outfit, for the serious meeting days. Here is her art gallery dress, the one she wore to that Christmas event, that worked on the hapless, intoxicated employee. And here are her surrender pants, the ones that signalled the official retirement of the lower half of her body.

All of these—she looks—all of them are not right. They aren't her. And she is so tired of spending her days as these people.

Aris is crying onto her herringbone skirt; tears drop onto her crepe-de-chine funeral dress. Her little chain-handled purse contains a kleenex, which she uses before throwing it, and the purse, against the wall.

A cat jumps overhead.

Crap. All of it. Can't even give it away. What poor woman in Darfur needs her fake Chanel? Who wants a skirt with a diagonal bias cut when clothes are falling off and open sores are running?

Ugly belts and too many shoes.

Too many shoes.

The cats scurry and tumble. They are happy in the sudden chaos, as cats are. Aris nurses a raspberry green tea, the tang and bitterness bracing. She is wearing blue fluffy slippers. Look at them. Look at her.

The taxi costs her thirty dollars. She buzzes once. Twice. The moon is not visible but the lamppost light is okay. Bugs like it. She is giving up when the buzzer is answered by the pulse of another buzzer. Aris opens the door. It is otherwise silent in the building. Three a.m. has that effect on people. She hears a creak and a groan as a door cracks down the hall. Aris's running shoes are undone. Her face is pinched from crying. Then, from around the corner, the moon appears.

"There you are," he says, and lets her in.

Aris awakens to an unfamiliar grouping of stars. She can just see out past the tree; an early morning sky. The stars are fading back into the firmament. A day-blue blanket is tucked up to her chin. She is a baby. No, a child.

She is a child here, in this bed, peering out over the wooden window shutter.

Where has he gone? Aris remembers arriving at his door, the hallway's overhead lights making her feel like she was in a 1940s movie, her running shoes out of place.

There was tea, a pot of it, and he had sat with her.

He sat through all of it, without asking for the going rate that Dr. Grogan demanded.

Is it wrong to lie down when one is tired? Is it?

He told her to. Put your feet up. Lift your feet.

She was thinking of the Chagall hanging in the gallery, the feet so weightless, people floating over villages, love brimming from eyes and fingertips.

When there were no tears left, she lay there looking out at the stars. The moon-faced one made a place for himself in the living room, leaving her door open and just staying in her orbit. He reflected in his corner while she floated.

Her grandmother told her about men with brooms who used to sweep the sidewalks clean at dawn, and wash down the front steps of shops, all before the streets came alive.

That was England, and that was then.

And *everything is tickety-boo*.

She can see him on the couch, his spectacle-less face peaceful. Here, in this Spartan life, this semi-dark apartment, here with an injured body, Dunstan sleeps. And is at peace.

Aris floats. The traffic begins. Water starts running through pipes.

That the world can be the same as it was yesterday. That it can possibly be the same.

"Skivvy! Get a move on!"

Skivvy. Concubine. Mort. We have all been called forward. On deck, I can see Captain Ward speaking to the officers. The crew, too, has made ablutions, as much as is possible at this stage of the journey. There are comments flying about concerning the governor of this place, Macquarrie is his name.

"He's as new here as you are," a mate fingers my hair.

They are joking about Bligh, the former head of the colony. Poor man lost his boat, and then came here and lost the continent.

"Aye. Rum Rebellion, and didn't he go an get hisself arrested by his own people! Fair useless piece...."

Silence.

Captain Ward moved down the line. His buttons are shiny. He is speaking now, of the journey, of the one lost over board. He has not mentioned the babe that did not survive its birth. He wishes no further numbers in the record book.

Cord tells us that we must all adapt to this world, New South Wales. It is to be our home. Our prison and our home.

And it begins. The headland is sandy, like Marsh's hair. It is, like his face, sun-kissed and filed with light. I see bits of colour, shrubs as mother might dig up out of the garden, their green not green enough. Birds scream overhead.

"What are they?"

"Cockatoos," someone answers.

A mate adds, "Thems galahs. See?"

We are going in.

O, Mother, it is like falling into a dream and being afraid to let go of the shape and the smell of the bed, holding on for as long as possible.... I see Caroline's brave face. A smile. And I let go and fall in.

We sit at harbour, land so near. How long will we be here like this? Cries from shore reach us and some of the women wave. We are not to go right in, is all we know. We are to sit on this piece of wood. How many days?

We are sent below. Cord and others try to keep order.

We wait.

Night is dreadful. I feel the spirit of Cassie Jukes among us. Caroline holds me and tells me the story of a room filled with books, a grand library. I ask if she has ever seen it and she looks wistful, as if she might have.

The next morning we await the opening of the hatches. Cheers, whoops and the assorted noises reach us.

"What is it?" Cord calls.

"Boat rowing out!"

The faces down here are foolishly happy, as if freedom is approaching with every pull of the oar. We are lined up again. It is our descriptions they want. Have they not known us? Are there no lists?

Caroline is with me.

They look at Hettie Rags Crenshaw. They have her down for fifty years but she could be more ancient.

"Eyes?"

"Two," she mutters and is about to be reprimanded when the official realizes she has misunderstood.

"Right," the stern young man says. "Tattoos? Other marks?"

Whispers run through the group. Some have taken it up on board, and there are a few that would best remain unseen.

"Tattoos?"

Hettie unleashes a stream of invective and is pushed roughly. A cursory examination of her arms reveals nothing but flea bites. She is put aside.

Caroline is next. They note her dark hair, dark eyes, her stature. She says nothing, for she is still listed as mute.

"Complexion: fair. This one doesn't look too bad. Make a note."

They note her eternal beauty and the scars on her ankle.

"Right. We've a place for her. *And* she's a mute," the official says, noting the keen advantage.

When is Harkness going to speak for her? He surely will try to have her placed in Sydney, where he can see her and come back for her.

I am the next in line.

"Quell, Maura," he says, dipping extra ink when my "Q" dries up.

My stature he lists as average. My hair does not impress, and my eyes, though clear, are not deep pools as the poets admire.

Complexion: clear. Rash on cheek.

Condition: sturdy.

I believe he thinks me a pack mule.

"Tattoos?"

If I had had one I would have gone for the man holding the anchor. I CARRY MY HOPES WITH ME is what the mate had told me.

"None," I reply.

"Show me the arms."

My arms are brought forward by the other officer, my clothing pushed back.

"Elsewhere?"

Why does he do this? Did he hear my remarks earlier concerning the treatment of some of the simpler members of our band?

I feel the official's hands upon me, reaching....No.

"Right! We'll have order!"

They stand while one removes my dress and I am only in my shift. The boat is silent. Only the birds comment on my bitten skin, my bruises. I know this feeling. I look up and blind myself with the outlines of birds.

The sun smells damp. How long do I stand? Mere moments, as they peer and poke. The sun has my eyes, now boiling in tears.

When I bring my head down to their gaze, to the boat, I am shocked. There is Caroline. She has lifted her own dress over her head. She stands in her shift beside me, her nose high.

I look.

Now Hettie Crenshaw, all the decaying layers of her, is pulling at a knot of rotting fabric, and what is more gripping is the demented grin upon her face as she does so.

It is when I see Cord step forward and begin to untie her apron that my heart gives way. Our roar is such that Captain Ward himself appears. Words are spoken. The officers return to the forecastle.

I shiver in the sun. I have no words. I look at Caroline, and nod to Cord. I help Hettie Crenshaw back into her webs and strands.

"Bleedin' beetle," she says, "perfumed little prick as I…."

Harkness speaks to Caroline. They stand off to the side. The shipboard couplings are over as we have arrived and must now resume our natural places in the world. But Harkness has requested that Caroline be placed in a good home in Sydney, so that he may claim her when his service is completed.

Caroline returns to me. She has hopes of our being placed together, although such a thing is highly unlikely.

"Nearby, then," she says.

She wishes to give me something. She would give me her shell, but having lost one already, she feels she cannot part with this one.

"I don't know that he would believe I could lose two."

I, as well, have nothing for her.

Yet we have heard of the blending of blood, the ritual that makes men brothers. Had I still been able to enter the surgery, I could have provided us with a means. I ask a mate who is splicing rope if I might borrow his blade.

He laughs.

"Do I look mad?" he asks.

We are prisoners, after all.

I tell him what we mean to do and he offers to stand by. Caroline's palm is not as smooth as it was back in the prison. Nor is mine. We wipe them clean.

As it is my idea, I go first. I find myself wishing it were a keener blade than one which hacks at ropes.

A line like a closed eye. Then a red teardrop.

She takes the blade. Her movement is swift, and she is also bleeding.

"Well…we should say something. I…should say…."

The mate watches. And there is nothing to think of. We look at each other and press our hands together in friendship. Our blood mingles as we stand facing one another.

"We shall stay…," I begin.

She continues with her eyes.

"That's me knife if you don't mind."

The piebald birds fly, the boats approach to take us ashore.

I stay close to my originals—Cord, Caroline. We are minus one, of course. One who is treading the roof of Hades.

I watch as they assist Izzy Watts over the side. Surgeon Matthews supervises. He will not look at me. He is in full uniform and looks the splendid gentleman that he is not. I think of his poor wife at home, the many months apart, how she knits and frets and will welcome him home to her bed.

Cord is beside me. "I've heard if you can get assigned to a decent place it's better here than back in London."

O, London. I have not thought of you, except in despair, sadness over the boy. Eugene. My desertion is complete. I have put an ocean between us, my own brother, my little boy.

They are pointing at us. Cord. Caroline. I look at the ship and see it rise above my eyes as we descend. I think of the string wrapped around Cassie Jukes' wrists, her belated struggling, the stupor, the clouded vision of a boat rising above her as she falls.

"Oy! You! Into the boat, now!"

The ship, once so unsteady, is the earth to me now, the lighter moving precariously. Caroline is in. Cord beckons. Hettie Crenshaw frays above me, so I have no choice. I let go. They bundle me into the boat. Caroline reaches for my hand, two girls out for a punt along the Thames.

The continent awaits. We are all breathless but for the rowers who grunt and start out. The world opens out ahead of us. The trees are greenish grey, or red. I know trees and these are new, the way they stand and gesture.

Cord has heard that there are animals here the likes of which we have never seen. She engages one of the rowers to tell us of them, their names as strange as their descriptions: wallaby, kangaroo, echidna, platypus, wombat.

"Finally, a name for you," Hettie Rags Crenshaw clucks at me. "You seem a wombat. 'Wotcher think?"

Caroline laughs but says nothing.

We are moving in on the harbour, the cliffs are moving as well.

"They're all waiting for you, ladies," the rower grins, plunging us back into uneasy silence.

A roar arises that rivals that of the shipmates when we first saw land.

The bodies look like dolls, lined up on the shore. They are no bigger than my thumb. Why do I fear them so?

It is a parade they want, a trooping of the females past men who are drooling after us, pointing and reaching. They are making sport of it, calling out, bidding and jostling. A shoe is thrown high; someone starts a fistfight. A wee boy walks alone by the water, nobody watching him. He is unsteady on his feet.

Men with monstrous beards.

Men in serviceable clothes.

Men.

Caroline has been spotted. A gentleman gestures and calls for an officer.

He is serving another client who cannot work the microfilm reader. He is patient, as always. He has not changed.

"Aris, hello," he calls out, in a voice too loud, too alive, for this room.

A snicker from Bruce, wheeling by a cart of ancient monitors.

Has he? Has Dunstan also felt the awkwardness Aris has insinuated into their relationship?

Relationship!

Dunstan comes over to her terminal.

"Hi," he says. His eyes are a bit red. Allergies? She doesn't know much about this fellow.

"How are you feeling?"

Aris looks at his ink-stained fingers; the same hand that placed a facecloth on her forehead.

"Okay," she says.

He has some sites ready for her to peruse. He's also found an old hardbound copy of a settler's diary.

"Always good for clues," he says.

Bruce passes by with the empty cart. "Hey, Birthday Boy," he says. "I'm finishing the cake."

"Why didn't you tell me?" Aris almost yells, holding back only when a head swivels.

"Uh...you had other things on your mind."

"When...when I...you mean *that* was your birthday! The other night?"

Dunstan smiles ruefully.

"Look, I am *so* sorry," Aris says, angry at being in this position in the first place. Why didn't he say something?

"Am I that bad?" she asks. That lame? That much of a mutant? "Can you not trust me with the information?"

Again he smiles.

"I don't have a gift for you," she says.

"You do," he puts his hands on her shoulders and draws her attention to the screen. As she familiarizes herself with the site, he leans in and says, quietly but clearly, "I've decided you're going to teach me about the human heart."

The Parramatta Female Factory. She would be there. The paintings of the original buildings are representations of despair. Would they give her a decent place to sleep if she went into service? Would they keep her from harm? The Convict Indent said she was sent to the Factory and then to a household. Maybe she married and has descendents.

My descendents?

Aris pauses. Because, of course, she doesn't know.

What does Dunstan want from her? She knows what keeps a heart going, the artificial stimulants and hardware that prolong the life of people whose own hearts have been betrayed. Whose hearts have betrayed them.

Her grandmother, sitting in the living room, playing the tiny upright piano, still blistered inside from old wrongs, slights from family members long gone. The piano out of tune, the melodies dusty and flat.

What can she tell in about the human heart?

It plinks. It is out of tune.

Her eyes are numb. Is this physiologically possible?

He meets her on a Saturday afternoon, liquor store bag in hand, a fleece throw over his arm.

"Picnic," he says, instead of hello.

Aris doesn't know why she has consented to this non-research-related outing. She has things to do. Her apartment needs a good turning over, for one.

"I thought we could walk down by the river until we find a good spot."

If he is up for it, who is she to say no? She has a pair of walking shoes on, not cheap ones either. It would be nice to justify that particular splurge. They pass arrowhead fern in the water, and ducks. Some kind of a climbing weed—jimson? —is taking a tree down leaf by leaf, suffocating it, pulling it in and incorporating it like some crazy BORG on *Star Trek*.

No more Space Channel, she vows.

Aris finds herself getting into the leisurely pace of this walk. Dunstan is still moving with caution, so they have the excuse to pause and examine rocks, flora, moss. The sound of water lapping against the lip of the land reminds her.

"Do you think we'll ever find her?"

Their girl, notwithstanding.

Dunstan looks at her, and she sees a red-faced, moon-faced man with a comical cotton hat and a liquor store bag.

"Of course," he says and leads on.

They have eaten the pita and hummus, the tabouleh and the crudités. They are full of garlic and full of sun, and the Nanaimo bars sit untouched.

"They'll melt," Aris suggests.

"With that sugar, though, they'll last forever, in one form or another."

What is she doing here? What, for that matter, is he doing, spending his day off with her?

"I like you," he says, reading her thoughts. He'd better not read all of them. He'd best not get to the part about the soon-to-be middle-aged man with no life, no girlfriend or partner, a medical condition rare at his age that might prove a major complication, a man with a round child's face that shines….

"Sorry. I just…thought you should know."

He picks up and over-examines a stone. Geologists do a more cursory job. He stands and flings it with surprising dexterity out across the water where it skips not twice but three times.

"Not bad," Aris stands, searching for her own rock. But she angles it so that it takes two dumpy bounces before sploshing into the river.

"I knew a kid who could do six," Dunstan says.

"Yeah, we all did."

They sit together watching the ducks. Aris feels the reflection on her right.

"So…," she says.

"Yeah," he says.

This is not normal. Normal people meet, are attracted to one another, give their personal and sexual histories, and jump into bed. Instead, Aris is tongue-tied for a freakin' word, here. She can imagine the bus chorus.

Fake Gucci bag:[You're on the bus, honey!] "Did you see the strange couple that just got off?"
French manicure:"The old-looking guy with the woman?"
Gucci:"She had O/C disorder. And he looked like he should be selling pencils somewhere."

"What I mean is…."

He is trying to give her an out. He has his sword positioned and is about to fall on it. He has been too good to her for that.

"I know what you mean," Aris says.

A jogger huffs by behind them.

"Oh," he says. And is done. It is up to her.

Aris stands again and stretches her legs. She walks close to the shore. A crayfish is dying on a styrofoam tray.

"Do you know," she turns," do you know that you're a good person?"

Does any of this filter out into space to reach the moon of his face?

"Oh," she hears him whisper, "a treatise."

Something painful possesses him.

"Dunstan...."

"Present," he says, smiling back into his placid safe expression. He could disappear forever, like Maura Quell. Why the hell doesn't he stand up for himself?

"Dunstan!"

"What?"

"I..."

"What, Aris? You see, I know the rest. I've heard it before. I've been here, you know? Right here. Sometimes it smells like garlic and sometimes it smells like coffee, but I have heard it all before, so if you don't mind...."

In her madness, she steps forward.

In her state, she takes the round orb of his head into her hands and kisses the angry lips to quiet them, to stop the words she has heard so often, has said so often.

In her madness, ducks are wading at her feet.

And then, stasis. Sanity returns and now she is as close to Dunstan as she has been to anyone in fourteen months.

Oh no. She backs away.

His face, while not transformed, is embellished with an expression she can't read.

"Whoa, geez...," Aris says, to clarify.

There is remarkably little to discuss on the return walk. Dunstan finds a garbage can and dumps the bag, throwing the remaining pita bread to the gulls. Aris walks behind, dutiful wife, dutiful servant, child in tow. She is too afraid to walk beside him.

Yes, Dr. Grogan. I have screwed up Big Time. It isn't a question of giving Aris a push and sending her out into the world, is it? Her brain should be a registered weapon. Hasn't the man, Dunstan Regimbald, confessed that he wishes to learn about the human heart? Isn't she, by default, the heart expert, able to speak of puppet hearts and pacemakers in the same breath?

Puppet hearts. All she is good for.

He plods on ahead. What is he thinking? Is he buying a hide-a-bed in his mind? Is he embroidering pillow slips?

Aris, was it wise to confuse so confused a man?

Dr. Grogan is sighing and raising his glasses up to the top of his head.

"Dunstan," Aris calls, for he has gotten quite a bit ahead of her. He pauses, turns around, his face a mess. But he waits. They continue together in silence.

She just needs a couple of days to herself. She needs to think this out. The bloody cats are gamboling. She actually, occasionally, feels sorry for them, cooped up alone in the apartment all day. They never seem to go out, are always eleven or twelve feet above her head.

In a few days she will go in. Or she'll call. Maybe he'll call. He has his pride, as well. He has to Save face. Such a child's face. Trusting. Open to it all, especially pain.

Aris has reached a point in her life where she doesn't want to be involved in anyone else's pain. That's it, isn't it? A Eureka moment, as Dr. Grogan and Oprah say.

She doesn't wish to hurt anyone. She would like to be neutral like Switzerland, inert like helium. She would like to tick along like a healthy heart, oblivious of the pains of that other heart, the one that constricts when it hears a name that bleeds when it is betrayed.

To be only the pump.

But where would that leave Maura Quell? Aris has coaxed tidbits out of files and proceedings. Maura exists there, on the boat, there, in the harbour, because Aris insists that she does. Because she wills it, employing her own heart to make Maura's beat. Turn away and the girl disappears.

Leno is blabbering on TV. Aris will be glad when he retires to his motorcycles and cars, relics of the gas years.

Work is becoming impossible. Aris has taken to coming in early. A quiet office. Even the ride in is not the same.

He: I can't believe it. Here they go again. Five hundred jobs.
She: Every year it's the same. We just get one assurance and they stick it to us again.
He: My daughter's finishing high school this year. I don't know what to tell her about university.

This serious lot, also heading in to work for the moment, has no time for bus banter, seat saving. They are good servants, well-dressed, deferential. They are the perfect people to take their own job cuts with grace.

Nobody in the office. Aris gets the coffee going and throws a trio of green fuzzy things out of the refrigerator. She is looking at the latest info-dump from the boss. Aris stands in her cubicle. The photograph of the Rose Bowl Parade is crooked on the fabric wall divider. Aris rips it from its place.

And this acrylic pencil holder.

She doesn't even have a pencil here. Yes she does. A mechanical one that is missing its lead.

Out.

Her drawer contains, among other things, a wrapped wedding shower gift for Ginny, last year's part-timer who broke up with her fiancé prior to the engagement party.

Out.

Wait! What if it's something useful?

Aris vacillates and lets it drop.

Okay, so maybe the appointment with Dr. Grogan isn't necessary. She just wants to get a few things on paper, is all.

"So, Aris. Sit down. Why don't you tell me how you've been?"

Aris settles in.

People get paid to listen to you, to remove your corns. To open up your heart. For a price I will open up your heart. I will put things inside, clever things as I have invented.

"Well, Aris, really, I can't make decisions for you. Are you sure it's the right time to start a new venture? If you feel it strongly, then perhaps it is."

Doc, I really have to sacrifice turtles right about now.

Well, if you feel strongly, then perhaps it is the right thing to do.

"Didn't you tell me I should start living?"

"Well, yes. But I didn't say anything specific."

Poor Dr. Grogan. What a strange job it is to bring people to the Promised Land and not to lead them into it, like Moses, a forty-year intern who gets canned the night before the big move to the office with the window.

"Well, let's talk about the rest of your life. How is your hobby coming along?"

Aris has a flash, a vision of a leg in a shackle, just the leg, lacerated, rubbed raw. She has no idea who owns the leg but the sight of it makes her flinch.

"Aris?"

"Swimmingly," she says.

The ship rocking, the bodies climbing down into bobbing-cork boats.

"That's an accomplishment. Good work! Pat yourself on the back."

Aris looks up. Does he actually expect her to do it?

"Anything you'd like to talk about regarding relationships? Anything on the horizon?"

What does New South Wales look like?

"Prison," she mutters.

Something skitters across his face. But he's good, masking it with a sudden sniffle.

"Are you in contact with someone in prison?"

Dr. Grogan's reputation is on the slippery slope, here, as patient number 15 takes up with a serial killer—conjugal visits, a murderer's issue popping up hither and yon for the next twenty years.

"Thanks for your time," Aris says.

He wants more.

Thanks for your help, for your mixed metaphors, your slightly patronizing approach? Thanks for looking at me and seeing a middle-aged woman but not seeing the menopause part. And thanks for suggesting dubious alternatives to my soul-deadening life.

"Thanks for inspiring me," she says.

And dear Dr. Grogan, he is just so happy. All it takes is a little encouragement.

Bus Fun
Elderly woman: You started up before I was properly seated.
Driver: Sorry, Ma'am. I waited, but the light changed.
Woman: I don't care. You people don't know how to drive. Don't they have buses where you come from?
Driver: Yes, and old ladies like you, Ma'am.
Woman: Old lady! I'm going to call and complain. What's your name, Driver?
Driver: Stupid immigrant shithead, Ma'am.

Aris makes a point of thanking the driver when she gets off.

O, Mother. O, Mum.

They gave us our places here in this penitent's hell. They looked and they touched, laying claim. They offered no hope. No pity. And I only had her, Mother, to keep my heart beating.

Cord was pushed off from us, and she is not near enough to speak with now. Poor Hettie Crenshaw will not last long, I believe, seeing how roughly they made with her person. And I felt, Mother, that I could endure anything. I could take it all and bury it beneath the overgrown roots of the hornbeam tree. And I could run home to you and Eugene, and Mary Lavender down the way. If I had Caroline.

When they came to take her it was a buzzing I felt, a noise in my head. There was talking, there was a settler with a pipe and a greenish vest. I couldn't hear them say it, for the buzzing; I could only see their mouths moving. I could see Caroline opening her mouth but nothing came from it, of this I am sure. She wished to speak but was cursed with dumbness.

She was a mute and, I, deaf to all they said.

They lifted her from our makeshift cot of straw and rags, pulling her up by the elbows. She began wailing then, in silence, her mouth open, her arms trying to clutch back at me.

I was on my knees. I was made of lead, my arm so heavy as I lifted it to her, my hand still healing from our blood pact. I wished to hear her voice but there was nothing but the busy swarming of wasps, the fluttering of paper, and Caroline was gone.

I have not moved, Mother. And do I not look penitent now, holy, on my knees in prayer? Kneeling in darkness, the wasps turning round in my head.

I am found like this. The guard calls out. "You. *Canada*. Name?"

How am I to tell him, I....

He lays a swipe across my back.

"I said, name?"

"Qu...Quell."

"You *Canada* lot."

Even here there are divisions. Those pregnant or with babies are kept together. Those suitable for marriage are lumped as one. This is where we were told we would go. But Caroline has been taken into service. She has gone to a house in Sydney. The words come through the buzz as I hear them say it.

She is gone from this place.

Now they would have me in with the worst lot.

Cord is taking care of the mothers.

I will be with the dangerous, the old, or the mad. Hettie Crenshaw lets out a cheer when I am brought over. Yes, Mother, I made some friends in London.

Dust. Dust, my eyes.... I am blind....Damp, sweat, oil....

Muffled cries. My face, I can't....

How many arms and legs?

A fly...fly on a window. Beating, wings, now on its back, legs, black threads fighting. Fly, fly...!

Kicking out.

Threads crawling, eyes, legs of glass.

Out. Out. "Out!" my voice.

"Right...she wants out."

"Wants you out, you mean," a laugh.

Cackling, chuckling, picking, barge poles, eyes, threads, only threads. Threads and dust.

It is Hettie who finds me. The dried straw or grass, Parramatta grass. Dust in my one open eye.

"Oy! Over 'ere!" she shouts, leaning in, her spider-web shawl across my face.

If there is a report, I know not of it. They see me as incorrigible, an unrepentant convict.

"Your depravity is a poor example," says she who is our devil here. The guards nod. They look upon me. I smell them.

"You. Take her over there and sit with her while she sets herself right."

Hettie Rags Crenshaw takes my arm. We walk the same way now.

"Right…them bastards is not what you're about. Over 'ere… ye kin rest a while."

Only now do I feel the bruises. I cannot…control….

"Right. Look, I'll find ye sumpin.'"

I am already on my knees. It is not so far to fall.

My body is not my own. I burn.

When she returns she has a cloth, a pair of…she has undergarments.

"How…?" I see then that she is without her shawl.

"That one there, mad as Tuesday, she's the one as got the cloth and water. And never you mind about the rest."

I am ministered to by Hettie Crenshaw, who carefully washes me.

"Same as me, luv. Me mum told me to lie on me side for a bit. I know it hurts. Nowt for that but time."

She sits by me. She is no comforter, Mother.

Mother, I am sorry.

I am sorry.

As I close my eyes, your hand reaches for my forehead. I fall forward into a field of flowers and I hear Hettie tut-tutting, drawing her blunt claw through my hair.

Sewing in this light. My eyes ache, and there is something on the breeze, some flower, that makes my eyes itch and water. We sew garments. We sew our own tatters, and things as are worn or used by the settlers. Some of us are weaving Parramatta cloth.

I am thinking of a cambray shirt.

And I think of Caroline. I hope her time is better. Perhaps she is getting on in her new service. Perhaps Harkness has made his intentions official. She is clean, now, her hair, her nails. They will have tended to her ankle.

They are lining up the suitables for another parade. The carts arrive and out pour settlers, some well heeled and in need of a servant, others looking to wed and breed.

The chosen group is presented, walked round in a strange kind of dance. It brings to mind a ritual from long ago, a dance from the court of a queen. Here, the women move in a row, the men dropping handkerchiefs at those they are after. There is one…Sarah? Sarah Moseby? There is another, an Irish…it is the one from the boat, from that night. She looks down at her feet, then at the stocky settler, bends and picks it up.

She will be married.

This continues. Three more are to go into service in houses in Sydney.

One settler has spotted me.

"Her. What about her?"

I shrink back into the shadow.

"'Ello! Got to make it known, I'll not do any skivvy work!" Hettie Crenshaw shouts.

The guard shoves her to the ground.

"Her!" he points. I know those hands.

Then Matron speaks up. "She's not on our recommended list, Sir. She's what we call incorrigible. Hardened, is she. She's under lock and key."

"Too right. That one is what give me this bite," the guard adds. And how did he get it?

"Let me have a look at her. Stand up, you."

I stand.

The man looks me over.

"She'll do. You, girl, that's your name?"

I feel Caroline's hand in mine. "Maura Quell."

"Quell…can you work, Quell?"

"Sir?"

"Work…in a house. Can you keep house?"

And, Mother, I am thinking of our kitchen, and of the hearth and the chair.

"Have done," I say. "Can do."

"Right. I'll take her. My wife will be wanting a servant and someone to help with the children."

There is some muttering I cannot make out. And it's done.

I don't see Cord or I would say goodbye.

Hettie sputters on about something. The guard hits her again and I step between them, he with my teeth marks on his arm. He glares at me, arm raised, and then grins, blows foul breath into my face, and retreats.

I lift Hettie from the dirt. Her face crumples like her dress.

"Oy, leave me me dignity," she shrugs off my hand.

I see her tears as she turns away.

✤

She hadn't expected to do it. It started out as a pathetically normal day. Cats clawed at her head, the water wasn't warm, toast was stuck, and she got to stand on the bus in to work. She didn't know there was anything different about the day, but there was, and whatever it was, she responded accordingly.

"Quit? Aris, sit down and close the door."

The boss puts on a real show of concern. It is hard to take him seriously, though, with the miniature monkey on his desk. Ceramic, chipped, a gift from his child, Aris remembers. She wonders if it bothers Treener to see it there, testament to his life before her.

"Now, Aris, I know you've been needing some time off. I know I threw a lot onto the group while I was away. But it's like we've evolved into one little family, here...."

The monkey sits mute.

See no Evil? Hear no Evil?

"Really, could you let me know what brought this on?"

Speak no Evil.

What to say?

The wooden dummies watched the first artificial heart being built. Refinement after refinement, and then people who cannot feel, people who have forgotten how to breathe.

She will need a taxi with this box of office crap. Aris lifts the lid and notes the calculator, writing pads, gum. The service entrance is around back of the building and Aris heads there to deposit the treasure.

Free.

Three-thirty on a Tuesday afternoon. It was good of him to let her go directly. Perhaps he could sense the desperation? Yet she doesn't feel desperate. She is completely calm as she watches the bus pull up, as she files toward the back and snags a window seat.

She is breathing deeply as she passes the Thai restaurant and the shawarma place. She is distracted by the little boy who throws his hat into the street and the Filipino nanny who risks her life to retrieve it. The yellow of the daycare pinnies is a bright advertisement as the roped children file in a line to the Loblaws to look at the fruit.

She smiles at it, all of it, the toddlers pointing out colours and condoms on the sidewalk. Already her brain is sorting through the details. The rental property, steady all these years. The market. The phone calls. She will begin it all tomorrow. Today is hers.

Dunstan is at the doctor for test results. This, he has told her, will be his lot for the next several years.

If I have years," he adds, totally unnecessarily, she thinks.

Is he not aware that he has the glow of someone who has stared down death? There is that look. Only people who have imagined the world going on without them have it. It both ages them and makes them timeless.

Rain. Not just a spatter, or even a shower. Rain that means business. The windows at the archives look like the panels of glass at the aquarium in Montreal. Trees are fronds. How will she get home?

She is disappointed and relieved that he is not there. He has not left her any notes or clues. Aris finds that a little harsh. Maura shouldn't have to suffer for their foolish lapse.

Aris is perusing the document that lists servant assignments. It is not the most reliable looking site. There are missing dates, and it appears to be the result of one person's research, rather than an established project. Still, she sees the convict names pass by: Norton, Agee, Myrtle, Dotts, Lockett, Richard. Someone named Lexie Mac….

Maura Q….

Maura Q.

Assigned November, 1810. Family, Merriweather.
Maura Quell assigned to the Merriweather family.
Just as it said on the Convict Indent.

"Bruce," Aris sees him in the afternoon, his burger smothered in a gravy mess. "Hi...uh, how are you?"

This is awkward because Bruce has none of the social skills that would make it smooth. Neither has she.

"Uh...how's Dunstan?"

Bruce takes five salt packets.

"Why are you asking me? Aren't you two...?"

The thing is, Bruce doesn't get "awkward." He works it, plowing on.

"Aren't you two hooked up? Hah...didn't think I'd ever say that about him."

"No," Aris sputters. No, they aren't.

Surprise.

"That is, we're friends."

Bruce's grin is inappropriate in a workplace setting. Aris wonders if any of this matters on Second Life.

"He's okay. He's off today and then I think he's taking a week."

"Why...what's he up to?"

"How do I know? Ask him yourself."

Bruce slurps and then adds an extra squirt of cola to his glass before heading to the cash.

Answer your bloody phone. Aris's knee is jumping and it isn't because Caetano Veloso is on the radio.

"Damn you, answer," she says, just as he picks up.

"Hello?"

Breathe.

"Uh...hi. Dunstan. It's me. Hi."

His turn to decide whether or not to breathe.

"Hello."

"You were at the doctor's. How did that go? Was it good news?"

She realizes she fully expects him to say yes.

"He says the PSA is good, yes."

"Good. That's good."

Dunstan is shuffling something in the background.

"Dunstan?"

"Turning down the TV."

She can picture him there, his feet in those old men's slippers, resting.

"I quit my job today," she says. It just comes out.

Not a speck, not a shred of noise on the other end. They sit like that.

Then, "Why?"

The question she has been avoiding herself. She wishes there were a musical interlude on the phone, like the one she gets when she is calling the courier at work.

Where she used to work.

She has no job. "Jesus," she says.

Dunstan sighs. "Come over."

Merriweather. The family that took her in. Aris can't help herself. She imagines a family. Stern settler father; well, he'd have to be, wouldn't he? Transplanted Brit mother who never could have afforded servants at home in Meddy Auld England, now with her very own girl to push around.

A child or three. Three. Two girls and a boy who, if he is not of good character, will become pampered.

No. Not there.

But he gets his way, doesn't he? Maura Quell will dust and mop and perhaps be a lady's maid to Mrs. Merriweather. The lady, on second glance, is not without conscience, perhaps. She gives Maura something, an old hairbrush? A pair of used stockings?

Maura Quell. Do you sit in your tiny room at night dreaming of home?

Dunstan's vacation sounds like it will be uneventful. He has plans to visit the library, the agricultural farm and gardens, the gallery and a museum or two.

"You can come, too," he suggests.

She points to the plant on the corner of his shelf and he takes it into the kitchen to drench.

"I seem to have confirmed the Merriweather lead," she yells.

Dunstan returns, setting the plant down.

"That's good. Maybe there's something more you could do there. Aris…."

"What?"

"Do you want to talk about it?"

"What?"

"Your job. You not two hours ago told me you quit your job of how many years? Don't you want to talk about it?"

He can be so irritating.

"What's done is done," she says. Suddenly, the voice of her grandmother enters the scene and then the picture of the old woman at the piano. What is she thinking? Who is saying it, Aris or her grandmother?

Dunstan turns to her.

"I love you, Aris Sandall," he says.

What flows into her then?

"Why, you ask yourself, am I telling you this?"

She shifts so she can see the window over his shoulder.

"I…live like this. I don't know what will happen in my life but I have the feeling I don't have anything to lose. And it hasn't done me a lot of good over the years, I have to admit, but I tell the truth."

Aris examines her cup.

"So, Dunstan, what's the truth about me, then?"

"You," he sits beside her and takes her hand. "You are my friend. That much I know. And, you expect me to say that it's terrible that you quit. You expect me to frog march you back. But I can't, because you didn't make a mistake. And…as for me…the truth about me, about the way you are with me…is that I am your friend. I know that."

Aris has just allowed the man to let himself down. Good work, Aris. You have this honed to perfection. You now allow would-be suitors to reject themselves. You sit here drinking his tea while Dunstan Regimbald falls on his sword for you.

"I'm sorry," Aris says, capping an entire lifetime of passing the buck. *Sorry.*

Dunstan.

Sorry.

Dr. Grogan.

Sorry.

Mom and Dad, for not keeping you at home that weekend you went to Niagara Falls.

Sorry, Grandma, for not understanding the pauses between the words.

But I did get the words. I got Maura Quell.

"Dunstan, let's do some work," Aris says, and Dunstan turns on his computer.

I am shipped back to Sydney. I had but a moment to take it in before they had me on the way.

Cord pressed my hand. It hurt because of the healing wound. How long ago did Caroline and I press our red hands together? How very long.

But I am going back in the direction of Caroline. She is in a grander house, I am sure. How big is Sydney? Not as big as London. I will find her.

Like I found the boy?

I lose everyone I love, it seems, on the ends of street corners.

The air here is so strange. I must close my eyes and think very hard to see again the filthy streets, the clouds of smoke. Here is it blinding blue, and everything is drenched in light, like a shell on the beach. Like Caroline's about her neck.

The Merriweathers have two children, a boy and a girl. I am to help with them as well as perform such household chores as Missus deems appropriate. The women at Parramatta told me that the settler's wives are the worst.

"One step up from us, and all the more cruel for it."

The man what chose me seems upright enough, if cold. He is looking for a servant for his good woman, says he. He has, "no time for those as won't work."

I have always worked. They cannot take that from me.

Merriweathers: Chester and Isabella.
Children: Amanda and Nicholas.

The trip is best forgotten, like so much else. When we do arrive of an evening, I see the lamp lit and my heart jumps. I admit to it. I fall victim to my heart and cry at the sight of a lamp in a window.

O, Mother, I prayed it would be you on the other side of the door.

I am tired but I brighten my countenance when they let me in. A home. A woven mat, a picture on the wall. A mirror.

O, Lord.

A girl in a brown dress runs past the glass, flowers in her hand, racing to the cottage door. She is small, but solidly built. She is in the sun. I remember.

The person looks back at me, her awkward girl-woman eyes deep in her face, her brow rutted. She has a tooth going bad in her lower jaw.

"You! Quell!"

I look away. They all stare at me. The lady has a bit of lace at her sleeve.

"Quell, is it? Maura. Maura, I'm Mrs. Merriweather. You've met my husband. This here is my daughter, Amanda."

A sullen-looking girl not much younger than myself peers out from the settee.

"Nicholas, my son, is now asleep. You'll meet him tomorrow morn. I'll take you to where you'll sleep, as you must be tired. We'll set you up in the morning."

It's not a proper room, but an alcove round the back. Three-sided, with a curtain for a door. But, a bed!

"Don't want you sleeping on it 'til you're had a good bathe, mind. So for tonight you'll sleep on floor," she says, and I hear the London back alley in her voice.

I lie on the braided rug, a piece of rough cloth over me. There is a small high window, put there to keep the air moving. Tomorrow, when I am clean, I will stand on the bed and look out. Now, I lie down in the dark in the room. In my room.

They have a garment for me, a serviceable thick blue dress. It is too big for me, but comfortable enough. Stockings. Underthings. The shoes are more difficult to fit until they realize that Amanda's used pair will suffice.

I am shod, like a horse.

My duties are clear. I keep house, and it is a good enough house, three bedrooms, a hearth, parlour, dining room. There is a garden out back that is splendid.

The boy.

He was there this morning at the table. He is about six. He has pale blue eyes and fair hair, sandy like Marsh's. The boy's though, is curly. His body is thin and I wonder if he is ill, especially when they tell me that he is not six but nine. I look closer. There is something in his eyes.

The girl finds it amusing that I wear her old shoes.

"Mother," she asks, "Will she also wear my cast-off shifts and drawers?"

I work all morning, scrubbing a fine dust that coats everything in the house. I wonder what is beyond the property, and Parramatta, for I have heard that there are deserts, stretches of land so large you cannot take it all in, where you can walk for days without spotting another soul. I have heard there are mountains.

Some of the dust from those places is surely here, on this lamp with its many crystal droplets.

The shoes, which started out promising, have begun to hurt. The thing is, if I can do good enough work, if I can get them to see I'm trustworthy, perhaps they will allow me to accompany them into the market or to the main street, where I will try to find Caroline.

"You've left a dirty spot," says Amanda. She is a gruff girl, even with the bows. She could look pretty if she wished, but her pout puts an end to it.

She has books in her room. I would love to hold them, to read them, but I am not to touch anything personal, except in M'lady's chamber, where I am to dust all of her frippery.

The boy circles me, curious. Well, he does so with his eyes, while the rest of him remains in the chair.

"Miss," he calls me, though his family scoffs at the idea. His father, Chester Merriweather, is away all day, the mother has a hundred and one distractions, so there is the scowling wonder, the boy, and me.

"Miss…were you really…in prison?"

I turn, pushing my kerchief off my forehead.

"Yes, Nicholas. I was."

His eyes widen.

"And did they whip you and beat you?"

More images enter than my mind can stand.

"What? Oh, no, no, lad."

"Because my father says that the prison lot is worse than anything."

I place my feather duster—what are these feathers?—on the arm of the chair.

"Does he? Wonder that he should have me come here, then, isn't it?"

He nods, not taking his eyes form my face.

"Nicholas, are you really nine years old?"

Blue china eyes.

"But…well, you seem rather younger…do you know what I mean?

The boy shifts.

"Yes, miss. I was sick. I'm getting better now. Doctor wants me up and about soon."

I am surprised at how my heart leaps at this.

"Good! Good for you. And when you are "up and about" as you say, how about you and I go for a walk. Would that be nice?"

His eyes are charged at this idea. The first smile I have seen in Sydney.

177

Caroline. O, Caroline. Where are you? From my tiny window I see a tree and the cart road. Are you down that road?

The scar on my hand was pink when I finally removed all the grime. It took an hour to get the muck off, to unknot and clean my hair. We had to cut out a few bits.

The lady says I have got nits but I have not been scratching. She put something on my head. She scrubbed and picked. She was surprised I didn't have more fleas. So was I.

I watched as she kicked my old dress and shift onto a shovel to take out back and burn. The pattern on the dress so familiar, like my own skin.

But, I became clean.

And I lie in a bed, a real bed. The mattress is not a good one, not like the ones in the children's rooms, but it is my mattress.

I miss you, Caroline. I would whisper to you all of what has happened to me since you went away.

Are you happy there? Is Harkness coming back for you?

There is a moon that rises over Sydney. And they have their own collection of stars. It is so strange to see the stars. For while I saw them on the boat; I never saw them in London. This takes me back to the cottage. Here, the stars can almost speak, they are so loud.

It is only two weeks or so afterward that he finds my room. The curtain is a disadvantage, as it offers little privacy. I am glad for the curtain, though, lest things be worse than they are.

He points.

This is what he does.

He points as me and puts his hand over his own mouth, like a statue in a fun house. He points again and closes the curtain behind him. His hand is on my mouth, there, as the rest of him does what it does.

I knew.

O, Mother. Mum.

I have never had anyone kiss me.

The boy is by the window seat. He looks out at the garden the same way I do.

"When does the doctor say you can go out?"

"Doesn't. Hasn't."

"So…you could go out…today?"

He almost shudders at the thought.

"Today…oh, I don't think."

"Today is soon," I say, as I fold the coverlet on the arm of his chair.

He looks as if he wishes it more than anything, but his legs remain motionless.

"I'll go with you," I tell him.

A gasp escapes him.

And it seems with incredulity that he finds himself at the door to the garden. I push it open, for it sticks, and the world beckons.

"Step in," I tell him, and wonder why I do not say, "step out."

He places a careful foot. We stand there in the sun.

The flowers and trees nod at us. The breeze is from heaven itself.

"It smells good," he says, and puts his hand in mine, tickling the scar.

We walk around among the flowerbeds, the vegetable beds. At home it would be winter. Would it be winter? Topsy-turvy here.

"Not like at home," he says.

I am startled.

"Were you not born here?" I ask him, for I have assumed that they have all been here for many years now.

"No, I came when I was five. But I remember home."

He came once on a boat, as I did, having no say in the matter. He too dreams of another place when he falls asleep. Perhaps it will be his children, or grandchildren, who dream of here.

"Still, it's pretty, yes?"

"It's outside!" he laughs, and we make one more round before returning to the house.

We make a vow to tell no one, in case the doctor would have words. The boy's face is animated as he sits through the long afternoon. He catches my eye and smiles.

I nod.

179

It is a good week and then, again, the Master enters. He seems distracted, closing the curtain and fixing its pleats. When he turns, he again takes on the configuration of a statue, with his hand to his lips. Again he covers my mouth. Who does he think I will scream for? Who would defend me in this place?

He seems not to know I am here. He burrows and finishes and then he rises, a look on his face like he has just misplaced his gloves. He closes the curtain roughly, the hooks scraping across the rod.

The stars are bright. They witness all.

They are God's beams searching out the truth.

The boy played in the garden with his toy horse and cart. He let me handle one of his books and was surprised that I could read. I read him a story about a boy who fishes in a magic river.

✺

Aris has spent the morning on the phone with her financial advisor and the manager of her rental units. So many things to arrange when "selling up." Wouldn't Derek be surprised to know that she's managed to hang onto the small walk-ups this long.

Two modest rental units in an area Aris never visits, and she, across town, in an apartment of the same vintage. The apartments were to have been her nest egg, her hedge against time, illness or unemployment.

The egg is hatching, Aris nods, pulling out yet another file from the drawer.

Did Derek keep the other holdings? Or did he cash in his chips as soon as the ink was dry? She doesn't even know if he's on the continent anymore.

She's getting a sick feeling about Maura Quell. This past week Aris has not found anything. She has gone through many documents but has come up empty. Dunstan suggested writing or emailing universities in Australia to request searches. National Library. Maritime.

"It may cost you," he warns.

Aris antes up an apartment building, reminding herself that twelve families or individuals are being pushed to the center of the table.

She's cleaned her apartment and has been throwing away boxes of trinkets, bags of clothes. In the process she has come across the old leather photo album she was sure she'd lost decades ago.

My, my, weren't we a sweet family?

Aris remembers that dress on her mother, the blue wool not as soft to the touch as it looked. Her mother's hair perfect, always perfect.

Her own dress she remembers only as uncomfortable. Taffeta was definitely more of an idea than an ideal in children's clothing. Sculpturally elegant, it always made her feel like she was entering the dress rather than wearing it.

A Diefenbunker of a dress.

Her father looking into the back of the camera, fearless in his exposure to that keen eye.

How could they have disappeared in an instant? The semi-trailer was little damaged, according to the newspaper article. The driver was "shaken." And they were gone. Did her father stare into the oncoming vehicle the same way he stared into the camera? Did her mother take a breath in sharply, and never exhale?

Stuff and nonsense. Aris had trained herself years ago not to dwell.

And she hasn't, has she? Aris hasn't dwelled anywhere since. She holds the soft leather cover of the album and caresses it. Leather can feel almost as soft as human skin if you need it to.

The phone pulls her back.

"Hello. How are you?"

Mind-reader Dunstan Regimbald reporting for duty.

"Hi, Dunstan. I'm…adrift this afternoon. But the buildings are listed."

Dunstan congratulates her and asks when she will be coming in.

She doesn't want him to hear the disappointment in her voice.

"Oh," he says. He is definitely leaning toward settlers' diaries and university holdings.

"There may be mention in a diary. We have a family, after all."

There he is, like her grandmother, leading her on with a vague promise, in her grandmother's case, a threat. The piano, the row of relatives looking down, surprised to be encased in heavy, dusty frames.

He is silent on the line. What does he expect her to say?

"I'll try to make it in...I have to go over to the buildings yet."

"Sure. Well, okay then."

He hangs up and she can hear something in that click.

"If I could explain it, Dunstan, I would," Aris tells the overhead cats.

Amazing what one neglects. Doctors' appointments to make. Paperwork to do. And no Dr. Grogan to tut-tut her through it. No heart copy to write.

Your heart is shot. You may be eligible for a transplant, provided some young and healthy teenager road races next Friday night. Should said teenager sacrifice his life for you, you will be outfitted with a prime specimen, a heart barely broken, wounded only twice by girls in low-hanging pants and thongs, girls with tattoos that proffered Asian philosophies.

Tattoos. Aris is in the prime target group for an inappropriate tattoo. Just as Bruce is the prima age to enter into his seductive alternative Second Life.

She could get a tattoo.

She remembered the man with the bar code tattoo on his neck. He stood in front of her on the bus one day, waiting to debark from the back door. Aris wondered, then, whether he could actually be scanned.

She could get a tattoo.

But of what?

The bus is late, The new reality, with the recent influx in the ridership. They're all amateurs, but they take the place of the regulars. Literally. Aris feels for her old favourites, for the Seat Saver, who will be in a quandary for sure. Save a seat, sure, but for one of them?

Aris doesn't see that lot anymore, the going-to-work people. She is learning new routes, like the one to her properties.

The new ridership, she finds, is rude. They ride the bus like they own it; like they've a right to their extra bags and their inane questions that, let's face it, distract the driver; their pathetic stops called out in both official languages.

Google-map, *Dumbkopf!*

The buildings come into view. She wouldn't call them rundown, because they are not. But modest, yes, post-war pillboxes, six units each, one for the manager.

Aris sees herself in one of the windows, a woman of indeterminate years peering out from behind the curtain as the sign is pounded into the patchy lawn. How long would she have lived there? A decade?

The disruption, hopefully, will be minimal. The new owner might make improvements. But then, he'll raise the rent. Or raze the buildings.

What if she can't find a buyer?

Just like Derek to take the choice spoils.

"Ma'am," the property manager, Macklam, shakes her hand.

It will be okay. She finds herself wishing she could reassure the woman behind the curtain. *It'll be okay.*

Bus Fun:
Matron slumming: "You didn't give me a transfer."
Driver: "Lady, you didn't ask for one. I can't read your mind."
Matron: "Well, I'm taking the bus. Why wouldn't I want a transfer?"
Driver: "Perhaps you live at the transit stop, Ma'am."

Ah. We've come down in the world, haven't we, consorting with bus drivers, procuring little pieces of paper, standing in our heels and holding onto a strap? Perhaps, yes, sit there in the seat meant for the disabled, the mothers, the blind.

Seat Saver would have given you his seat. Know that. Seat Saver would have gotten up and given you his seat.

She can't believe she's doing this. The buildings will be sold. She has left her place of employment. There is a feeling that comes with pushing away from these things. It is definitely unfamiliar. She keeps being brought back to her parents, and the holiday weekend they left her.

Was it a wedding? They were off to something that she couldn't or didn't want to attend. She was with her grandmother. When she went to bed that night it was with the knowledge that they would return with a souvenir of Niagara Falls, something wonderful for her.

Her grandmother's sheets always smelled a little musty, like they'd spent a long time in the closet, but Aris didn't mind.

The sound of her grandmother crying out in the night broke into her sleep.

They were on their way home.

Among their effects, a thermometer with the Falls in the background, and a broken snow globe with The Maid of the Mist floating around, impossibly, in air instead of water.

Two of them at the piano, then, plinking out the old dirges. The boys, the bracken, the forests of England growing deep.

One thing left to do. But Aris is afraid.

In the vestibule of her apartment, Aris retrieves her mail. Three pizza brochures, lenswear, charity. A card.

Aris recognizes the handwriting. Pulls open the envelope. A mouse dressed in Sherlock Holmes gear, a large magnifying glass in his…hand? He's peering at a letter and is wearing a classic Eureka expression on his furry face. Inside, the clumsy verse reads: "By Jove, it's fairly plain to see, that I like you and you like me."

Dunstan has crossed that out and written on the verso side: "By Jove, Sandall, I think you've got it!"

Got what?

Aris has conceded that Dunstan can read her mind. It's when he reads it before she does that she gets nervous.

She is throwing the flyers and coupons into the recycler when the woman from upstairs comes by for her mail.

The Cat Woman.

Aris closes her detective mouse card, mutters a hello, and retreats.

📖

The work is not easy, but bearable. So are the taunts from the girl. She takes it upon herself to remind me daily of my mean position in this house. She gets this, I believe, from her mother, who is dismissive. Or from her father, who is cold and…. I cannot think of that wretched man, of his soul like a foul shadow about him. He has not even the grand evil spirit within him, such as could make one gasp at his power. He is a smudge, a low stench in the field. Something rotting.

The boy, though, proves a world unto himself. He reads to me while I work—this when no one else is about. He takes books down from his shelf. He would appear to be the only one who reads in this place, reading seen as something fit for the infirm.

I have been here, now, three months? It is hard not to lose track, for the days are the same. I still pray for market day and their eventual trust in me.

The boy was found out yesterday. We were in the garden. He was walking among the plants I do not know, standing taller than he has been, and quite proud of himself, too, when Missus came home. She was traipsing through the house to find me for some daft chore, when she chanced to look out one of the windows I'd just washed. She stumbled upon our happy secret.

O, Mother, I thought she was going to have my guts, she was so beside herself, ranting and the like. But the boy, Nicholas, he took her by the arm. He calmed her and that's when she looked him in the eye and fell into his wee arms. It is the first true act I have seen in this land.

They stood there, a garden statue for all interest and purpose, as I pulled up roots. After, Missus came up to me and put out her hand. I took it, and she bid me rise to my feet. She said nothing at all, nor did she smile, but her gaze was deep, as if she was seeing me, truly.

We went inside then and I busied myself with the girl's window sash. Amanda Merriweather has the best window in this house, the view wasted on her.

We are to go into town. Sydney! The boy must see his doctor and he has insisted that I accompany him. At first Mister disagreed. He never looks at me directly, but he nods his head in my direction when referring to me.

"Not her," he said, jerking toward me.

The boy put up a proper fuss and, amazingly, Missus took the boy's part.

So I am decked out in my too-large dress but without an apron, for once, and am being helped up into the carriage to sit beside the boy. Mister takes the reins; the girl sits opposite, with her mother.

"Now, Nicholas, mind you tell the doctor everything."

The girl stares at me.

"Nicky, dear, you must let him know how often you're fatigued."

The boy nods, but his head is turned, taking in the sights.

I, too, am distracted. To be out on the road, that road outside my tiny window, this fills me. What will we see?

Sydney is not London, but after the country house, the noise, the people, assault my heart. The buildings are not old and decaying, they stand proudly where they have been put. The shops are busy and there are horses and carts.

I saw a man of very dark complexion at the end of the street. He looked like he was asleep, except that his eyes were open. He reminded me of a post at the end of a long drive.

The boy demanded that I attend the doctor's appointment with his father, so Missus and the girl alight near to the shops. We continue on.

I sit outside the examining room. This room has a map of the world. I trace the journey I've made across the expanse of water. I make my finger bob along, the *Canada* crashing up and down in the waves. In the middle of the map I stop. I watch as a bundle slips overboard. There is barely a splash and the map remains smooth.

The room. A map, books, a water pitcher and fine tumbler. A brace of treasures, any one of which would send an unwitting person to Transport if taken. And if I took one here, would they Transport me home?

The boy returns, smiling. He takes my hand.

"He says 'all good,'" Nicholas says, looking to me, still six years old rather than nine.

"Good," I tell him, returning the squeeze.

Mister speaks with the doctor and then gestures for us to follow him.

Back to the bustle. He is to meet Mrs. Merriweather and the girl for tea. He would bring the boy, but what to do with me?

"I don't want tea," the boy pouts with new vigor. "I want to watch the people. She'll stay with me."

Mister looms. "She's a...."

He glares at me then, eye to eye. But he cannot hold the gaze, it seems, and drops it.

"She's not to be trusted," comes from his lips, but there is no heat in his argument.

"Look, father. We'll bring cakes and eat them there."

The boy points to the steps of a nearby building.

Mr. Merriweather ponders this.

"She's with me," the boy adds, comically.

Unbelievably, Mister agrees. He hands the boy a coin, gives me one more stern glance, and tells us we're not to budge from the steps.

"I'm tired, father. We won't go anywhere."

I turn to my brilliant companion and laugh.

"You've got it right. For I think you far more capable than I am."

I help him along the street toward the baker.

"Father can be easy," he says. "Mum as well."

"Amanda," I intone.

"Yes, she's the fly in the treacle."

We find cakes that remind me of those back home. The sounds in the shop make me want to cry. Voices from another place, smells and aromas from another time.

The boy says "tsk" and reminds me that it is not on to go all moody about a bit of cake. Nicholas makes his choice and we move over to the steps. Once he is settled he opens the paper and stares at the tarts, their jelly running out on one side.

"So," he says.

"So," I say, smiling.

We eat. I almost bend double at the taste.

Mother, did you make those tarts?

We sit as the boy makes his way through his sugared treat. He tells me the doctor promises him a full recovery. I have never asked exactly what was wrong with his little frame. It seems like he was stopped, somehow, in his growth. He is now back to rights, it would seem.

"I'm growing," he cheers, waving something sticky at me.

"Well, certainly your girth is after that."

"Did you like yours?"

For mine has disappeared faster than his has.

This lad. He gives me delight. I find myself thinking of funny stories to tell him, and his smile is what I look for when I enter a room.

We are there a while, perhaps a half-hour, when I look out on the market and see a figure by a cart horse. I stand. Crane my neck.

"What's wrong?" the boy asks.

I can't make out…the figure turns.

I am cold.

Caroline?

"C…Caroline?"

The boy rises as well, holding on to me, brushing sugar from his lap.

"What? Who's Caroline?"

My hands have gone cold. The scar is white.

"I…need to go over there."

I am already tripping down the steps.

"No! No, father said!" he cries.

The figure climbs into the cart. It is leaving!

I must!

"Maura, no! Don't leave me!"

His voice cuts me, stopping me. I am on the steps. The cart and horse retreat into the background painting of a town square.

Caroline.

The boy looks at me strangely, jelly on his lips.

I sit down.

How many times since then have I thought of her? She was the reason I burned the collar I was pressing for Missus. He'd scolded me then, and brought his nasty temper into my room, the curtain ripped aside.

She is the reason I stand on my bed and peer out of the window, down the cart road. And she the reason the boy found me in tears in the pantry.

He'd offered me his handkerchief, good lad. As I took it I thought of all the women who'd taken a handkerchief in the prison and gotten married. Or a handkerchief back home, and come here. Or a pair of breeches. Or a bit of braiding. Or a child.

I have been caught out pretending again, haven't I, Mother? As if I were a servant in a house. As if I belonged. Watching Caroline drive away brought it all back. I am a prisoner.

But the missus lets me out more often. She sees the way the boy is with me, and allows me certain privileges. The garden is one of our destinations. The boy is getting stronger for his forays out, his legs becoming, once again, used to walking, and his back appears sound.

One day she even suggests I go into town with Mister. She wishes me to visit the milliner and has a list for me.

He says nothing. Grunts his agreement.

When I am sitting up next to him and the road is before us he says, "Mind you don't try nothin' in town."

From this I believe that he means to let me out on my own. I am beside myself. I have not been on my own since before I was arrested.

I must not let him see me like this. He must not know or he will take it from me.

He too has things he must do. He consults his watch, places it back in his pocket, and informs me that he will return to the wagon in one hour. He does not tell me how I shall know it has been an hour.

But I shall. An hour floats before me, a walk into the forest, a game with Mary Lavender. A bread in mother's hearth.

First, I must attend to the list. The shop is not as grand as some I left behind. These very goods may have come across the water with convicts like Hettie Crenshaw, this ribbon floating to New South Wales with Cassie Jukes.

Each one of these, every strand of bead and ribbon, could have sent me here, could have got me whipped, branded. This pearl choker could hang a man.

That I have coin, now, in my hand, to place upon the counter, is passing strange.

The small packet fits into my bag.

Now I look out at the busy street. I am asea once again. I hold my breath, and dive in. London, cobbles, dust, soot. Here, a brightness, a tightness of the new. I have heard tell of the other who were here before the English. How do they feel, walking around these streets? They have made proper use without them all this time.

I realize I have been straining to see her. How odd I must appear. So I make an effort to calm myself, to walk as near to a lady's gait as I can manage.

There is a window I peer through. Along the wall is a row of books. I have only once before seen this many books, and they look from here like a pattern on a cuff, each row detailed like braid.

I turn round, then, and see her.

She is across the road, by a cart horse. Caroline?

What happened to you? For she is a copy of Caroline, an older sister.

I leap across, dodging a man with a cane.

"Caroline!"

She swings her head my way.

"Caroline…."

Her eyes. There is something clouding them. I take her hands. She doesn't offer them but does not object when I hold them. Her scar, too, has faded, but as I press her hands it becomes, again, visible.

"It's me," I say, peering. But the eyes are wrong. They are shallow.

"What has happened to you?"

O, Caroline, please.

"Talk to me."

She stands, mute, but a tear forms and falls down her cheek.

Where is Harkness? What has happened?

"Here." I take her by the arm and lead her to a stoop.

She weeps silently, even as her tears are mute.

"Where are you? What is the name of the family?"

I jump up and take a look at the cart. A package is on the floor, addressed to one Timothy Carver.

It is in my mind. I take, too, the place name and the street.

"Caroline," I say, holding her. "Listen. Listen!"

Her eyes rise to mine.

"I'll help you."

We sit, my friend and I, while Sydney moves around us, a honeycomb, and we two bees, identical to those about us, invisible.

I could stay here forever.

"You! Be off wi'ye!"

I am pulled by the hair and I snarl, swinging.

And a man, the man who took Caroline at the dock.

Her eyes. They no longer plead for anything. They no longer warn me. But mine are speaking. They are screaming now, Caroline.

They burn. I will find you.

Bruce is in the elevator. Someone has given the man a smart haircut. He looks younger, vital. Competent?

"How are you? Aris asks. She feels she almost knows him after all these months.

"Brimming," he says, a smile on his lips and...a song in his heart?

He gets off at Special Collections. He sweeps across the floor like a fast learner on that TV dance show. Maybe Bruce is a fast learner. Maybe he has caught up with that other Bruce, the one he could have been.

It's been a couple of weeks since she's been here. Things got busy with the buildings and the various paperwork that comes with freeing oneself.

Paperless generation, Aris clucks.

The Reference Desk is empty. She talked to Dunstan two days ago and he told her he'd be in on this shift, so she goes over to her terminal.

Someone is in her place.

Aris has to check herself from barging over and demanding her seat. The woman has her back to her, the short grey hair is serious, the striped shirt institutional.

Aris knows that she never signed in like the visiting scholars, that this terminal is not actually reserved for her. She feels momentarily adrift, standing in the center of the room. The large windows are filled with trees, pushing in, reclaiming the space.

"Aris!"

She whirls.

"Where were you? Lost in thought?"

The moon face is pale. A late night, early morning face.

She eyes her terminal.

"I know. It's a public spot, sorry. But the one near the window is empty."

Aris follows him and sits down at the far terminal. Too much reflection. How do people work here?

"Have you been okay?" he asks, as she sorts through her papers.

She just talked to him the other day.

"I was concerned about you," he answers.

"What are you, my mother?"

"No," he says, "But I'm working on her waist/hip ratio."

Aris laughs. It will be hard to tell him after all.

They sit up in the cafeteria. Posters of old exhibits grace the walls of this forgotten room. Dunstan squeezes a teabag against the side of his cup with a spoon.

"Not supposed to do that," Aris says.

"What?"

"It's just that it releases all the bitterness in the leaves."

"Says who?"

"I don't know. Tea Leaf Police."

"I don't mind bitterness. I like you."

He smiles.

Yes.

"I'm going away."

There it is, then.

"I'm going on a trip. A journey. You know I've been selling up. And so I think I need to get away and…."

"When?"

"Soon. Not right away, of course. Still doing paperwork. But I…."

"Where?"

"W5. Okay. I'm thinking of going to find her."
Who?"
"W5. Her. Our girl. Look, you said yourself that a lot of what I need to do now involves holdings over there. What's the use of sitting here and paying someone to search the holdings when I can go over there and do it myself?"

"Indeed. I have taught you well, Grasshopper."

"Ah, come on. You know I'm right."

He adjusts his glasses and looks out the window.

"Indeed."

Aris sits at the terminal but has no stomach for it. She watches him at the desk, pointing to the bay of reference books, handing out forms.

What had she expected him to say?

Jolly good, Aris. What fun!

Which reminds her of the card he'd sent her. What had he meant when he wrote, "I think you've got it!" Can he have known...?

She thinks of his apartment, the forgotten plant on the corner shelf, the leftovers she put in his fridge. So empty. So absent of clues, a challenge to any CSI.

The operation of the LVAD pump implants has become something of a medical mystery. The left ventricle assist device does the work of the heart until a replacement heart can be found. But in some cases the heart inexplicably heals itself, having enjoyed the 'vacation from work,' and recovers sufficiently to resume its full function. Scientists are both intrigued and puzzled by the phenomenon of why one heart fails while the other repairs itself.

Dunstan walks a woman over to the microfiche reading table, his body language almost genteel. Did he learn this in Clumsy College? Dunstan, graduate of Awkward Academy, is solicitous. Is that a half bow? The woman wants to read old newspapers, for Chrisssake! Look at him. Finger to the glasses. Ah, Spaz School.

Aris asks Dunstan if he wants to go to dinner.

"Korean," she suggests. "And maybe catch a film?"

The repertory cinema always has something on.

When he declines, she is not surprised. His health, a long day, their general awkwardness.

"Aris, I know you mean well. I know you wouldn't deliberately hurt a person…."

Is this true?

"But right now it's hard for me. You know. I am the default-keeper of my heart. Can't even give it away," he mutters.

The ride home is brutal. Kids on their way to a concert, an entire riot of them, take over the back of the bus. Swearing, body blows, music. The driver is oblivious. He'll drive them anywhere, to the edge of Heavyside crater on the moon for all he cares. There could be murders going on. The driver, in his hermetically sealed sulk, drives on.

She doesn't go back for weeks. Maura floats in space above her, when Aris is doing the dishes, when she is lying in bed. The faceless girl comes into view. There, the quirky smile that is rarely seen. There, the squinting eyes unused to the sun. Small for her age on the piano bench, feet not reaching the floor.

I know, I know, Aris tells herself.

She wants to tell Maura that it will all turn out okay.

I'm coming for you, she wants to say but she is afraid to voice it. Look what happened between Dunstan and her.

She has given notice on her apartment. There's something real in handing in a paper that says you don't want to live here anymore. Even the job resignation was easier, because most people dream of doing that.

- Hey, Bob, how's it going?
- Well, Augie, I'm on my way to hand in my resignation.
- No shit, me too!

But a home, however humble….

Her stuff will go into storage. Aris has contacted the storage company, out on a dismal road in the industrial section of town.

She'll need a large unit because, despite her apartment living and her recent purge, she has amassed a lot of crap.

Which she will leave to....

A large bonfire, perhaps. A smoke signal into space.

Cat Woman accosts her at the front door.

"I hear you're leaving us."

It is the "us" that lets Aris know she has made the correct decision.

"Uh...how did you...?"

"Oh! I'm going to be moving down. Your apartment's bigger than mine and I need the room."

Cheerful, this one. More space for her cats. More access to the mailbox, which she apparently patrols.

"Well, good luck," Aris says.

The woman remembers it at the door.

"Oh, yeah, you too."

Cat Woman has wished her luck. What more does she need?

Aris fights the urge to call him, to show up at his work with a box of fragrant tea. She is trying to be fair. So she packs boxes. Should she continue to carry the old letters, her grandmother's tatted doilies? It would be different if she had children, someone to put it all into context.

Which eventually forces her to ask the question.

What will she do with the genealogy? With Maura?

Nobody to leave her to either.

To find you just to lose you.

Maura. It is Maura she's thinking of now.

The boy reads to me as I dust down every surface. He reads well, better than me. He's clever, is Nicholas.

But I think only of Caroline. Since that day I have seen her twice but have been with the Merriweathers and, so, unable to speak with her.

The boy knows something is amiss. I cannot hide from him, for his illness has taught him patience and he has a keen way of observing all about him. Besides, he knows I can deny him nothing. I tell him, one morning, sparing him the worst of it. I tell him of our journey, and our bond.

He nods with an expression older than his face. I worry for him in this house, under the thumb of his brutal father. Of late, Mister has come to me full of rage. He is angry with me, it seems, and treats me with force.

I could not properly perform my household duties after one such visit, and her ladyship wondered what was wrong.

"Nothing, Missus. I'm feeling a little poorly."

She has little time for my ailments but she is concerned that she lose a servant in her new world. Her reputation as a lady of Sydney, in the balance, sends her for a country practitioner, despite my protestations.

I am made to submit to an examination. Missus is with me while it occurs. It is difficult and humiliating.

"Mrs. Merriweather," he says, and takes her aside to speak with her while I stand up from the bed in only my shift.

"What?" she thunders.

I am drawn back in. She is screaming all manner of foul words at me, words that were learned on the backstreets of London and not as lady of this house.

She has been told...she has been told....

But not he. Not his wandering member, no. It is I who am at fault, I who have been slipping out to find a drayman, a rancher. It is all on me.

"Foul mort you are," says she.

The doctor suggests a more balanced approach, but this is all he will offer.

And I am to be sent back. She doesn't want me here, with her boy, here, with her daughter a young woman now. Here, with her husband.

He echoes the thought, the head of the house. I am to pack my things. What things? I will be returned to the Female Factory.

My thoughts leap in two directions at once. Caroline. And the boy.

The boy who has been listening by the parlor door on his newly found legs, and who bursts in now flailing his arms and weeping uncontrollably. His small fists have little effect on his parents, but they break into me.

They open me. Boy.

He pummels me, hangs off my waist.

I put my arms round.

"Unhand my son!" the voice comes, crude and cutting like his body....

In my little room I drop to my knees. I have not prayed in a very long time. I have not read from the Book since I was on the ship. After what I did. Will He listen to such as I?

And yet, unworthy, I implore.

Am I speaking to the peeping stars? Am I pushing my words out past the branches of the tree?

Morning dawns too early. I am given a crust of bread and nothing else.

She, the girl, has arisen early to witness the spectacle. She twirls one tiny curl round her finger as I choke on the crust.

They will remove me before the boy awakens. Clever. They will take me the long way back to Parramatta. Dawn is just creeping up the fence as I shiver and climb into the wagon.

And I see him.

He is at the end of the drive. He wears only his nightshirt; his feet are bare. He should not be out like this. I look back at Missus but her early morning face is a mask of coldness.

"Settle in, you!" says Mister.

I hear the clop of the hooves and feel myself moving again.

The boy stands in the path, as defiant as he is able, his face red. His stares his father in the eye.

I would hold him and take him with me, take him from here.

"Move aside, boy!" his father commands.

The boy does nothing.

"Move!" The man makes raises his crop and makes to alight and the boy flinches but holds his ground.

"Now!" he cracks the whip.

Only when the mother, her nightgown dusty, reaches the boy and pulls him aside, do we move forward. I turn back to see his face. His mother has a hand clamped across his forehead.

He and I witness one another. It is all we can do.

The less about the journey back the better. He has nothing to say to me. As we make our way into town, the market is just coming to life. It is a grey day, for some reason. The landscape is almost flat, like a painting on a plate.

I am beside myself about the boy, and now, pressing through the center, where I have seen Caroline, I am torn again. We pass a home and I smell something cooking and my stomach growls.

He has driven us out past town, along a path I do not know. There is nobody about, under this canopy.

He turns to me.

"Right. You stupid girl," he says.

The birds burst forth above, colours flapping, and shriek when I do. His is big, and he moves quickly, but I am more agile than he. I kick at him, landing a blow to the chest and he falls backward, nearly toppling from the wagon. I am a step down when he grabs my shoulder and wrenches it.

Pain. But I slip through his grasp, down, and start running. Damned shoes.

He is heaving, coming after me.

The woods, Maura, how lost you can get in the woods.

His is coming.

He sweeps along like something possessed.

I outrun him, but he outreaches me. My hair!

He has me, my hair, and he pulls me back. I am scrabbling for the boy's gift, the little knife to cut flowers for his notebook, slim blade used on slimy stems. Small, fits in my pocket, in my hand.

His stench is above me, where his heart should be.

The little blade finds a flower. There is nothing, just surprise, as we both discover he has a heart. I pull away to let the red flower pool into my hands and not on my dress. The red revives my scar.

My blade. The boy's blade.

How long do we sit there, listening to the forest? Long enough to hear the special stillness rising.

Hide and seek, Eugene. It's all hide and seek.

I drag and cover Mister with a log and with fallen branches. I sit on the low branch of a fallen tree.

Strange and wonderful birds, cockatoo, macaw, parrot of every colour. This new land. This new, old land.

The horse will take me where I need to go. I have the destination. I am poor, but I am an honest settler, I am. Would you please direct me to the residence of Timothy Carver?

The town is busy this business day. I move through the people like a girl through the tall Parramatta grass.

It is a rich enough house. Richer than that of the Merriweathers. Perhaps I am mistaken? Caroline so pale, so lost behind the eyes.

I scout the property. They have a dog out front, but he looks to be a lazy old thing. I retrieve the scrap of crust just in case. Creep round to the back. Smoke from the chimney.

I look for the smallest window. But need look no further. Caroline sits in the backyard, at this hour, with a stick and a pair of boots. She scrapes the muck and hits the stick against a post.

I creep closer. I am almost upon her. There is only open space now.

"Caroline," I hiss.

She starts.

"Caroline!"

She sees me. What is it flashes across her face. Fear?

"Stay…stay there," I say, and hold my finger to my lips. Doing so, I see him again, pulling back my curtain.

I motion to her to go to the back of the property. Then I scurry there in the brush.

But she doesn't move.

"Now!" I raise my voice like Mister always does.

And she rises. Slowly. She walks to me, boots in hand. She looks like one of those statues in the other churches, one of the ancients, posing with hammer, or bread, or child.

Boots.

O, Caroline.

The leaves part and she is before me. I pull her in. I put my arms round her and she collapses into me.

My friend. My friend.

Sees the blood on my hands, despite my efforts to wipe it clean.

"Never mind," I say, come. Come with me."

Mother, you know I cannot get lost in the woods. Haven't you said I'm practically part of them?

Caroline is not going to be able to walk very quickly, but move quickly we must. The patient horse will take us. I am afraid that if Caroline regains her voice she will ask me where we are going.

And all I can think of is away.

In the Female Factory someone spoke of mountains beyond the river.

Blue…the blue mountains?

Blue Mountains. They sound so fair, like something out of the boy's fairy book. I should like to take her there.

Her ankle is not healed, my Caroline. She looks at me, now, and knows me. Presses her hand up to my hand, scar to scar.

This is a eucalypt, they say. But these other trees? The boy knew the names. He would tell me stories of the bush, things I will not tell Caroline. We're out for a Sunday ride, my dear, a saunter through Hyde Park.

We're pulling away from the world. Feel how light we are, Caroline!

"We're off!" I turn to her. For reassurance?

To reassure.

The animals scurry in our path, the parrots squawk their intentions overhead.

I will take her to the Blue Mountains. I will take her to the ends of the earth.

Aris has performed the Passport Dance, requesting priority service at a cost. Does this imply she is somehow more important than others in the queue? She can imagine the Passport crew, a pile of forms on their desks, a pile of sad, unsmiling faces, being required to separate those with RUSH standing.

Aris Sandall.

Asshole Sandall.

Candy Ass.

The extra fee is worth it, as Aris quickly has her passport in hand. It feels strange to be holding her passport again. The old one lived in the safety-deposit box until it quietly expired in its little metal coffin. She has only used it when she'd gone abroad with Derek, and how many years ago was that? All those pre-university plans to hitch-hike around the world had morphed into a tour of England, Scotland and Wales, accompanied by a group of seniors from southern Ontario.

But this is a new passport. Nothing here but her latest head shot, which reveals a woman Aris has a passing acquaintance with, one who shows up in the mirror before seven-thirty in the morning and then wisely makes herself scarce.

Fresh passport in hand, Aris decides to make a day of it. In the market is a travel shop that sells passport holders, travel togs and the like. Aris purchases a thin cloth passport holder that will fit beneath her clothes. She buys a compass because it is so quaintly compact, slipping into a small leather sheath. How do compasses work in antipodal Australia?

"Tilley hat?" the counter clerk asks, promoting the Canadian travel essential.

Aris tries on a few.

"So, where are you off to?"

Aris likes the brim. She pulls it low across her eyes.

"Oh...Australia."

"Oh, yeah? I have an online friend in Tasmania."

Aris hears but does not allow herself to think about this. Email pen-pals is not the Australia she is looking for.

Stopping for coffee in the market, she can't help but notice the bustle of the lunch crowd. Meetings, errands, a bite on the run, they crawl quickly, don't they?

Aris sips her tepid latte.

Her apartment is thinning out, bleeding out. Two boxes of CDs are going to the Sally Ann along with three bags of clothes. The Librarian Dress. The Surrender Pants.

Aris tries on her Tilley Endurable.

The women's shelter for her sweaters and shirts. Her linen.

Aris wishes she had some children's toys to put in with the shelter stuff. She decides to buy some to finish off the box.

Cat Woman will be taking over the unit. Aris imagines the place teeming with felines, cats settling into crevices and closets, sitting atop the refrigerator.

In the end, contrary to what she has assumed, she has only a small amount to put into storage.

Some family photographs. Who would want those? Her cousin, possibly, the stent woman.

Her job is long ago. A lifetime ago.

She realizes that the only part that made sense to her was the puppet man making his artificial hearts, Paul Winchell labouring on a replacement for the faltering human heart.

She is working on a replacement, as well.

And then she remembers what Dunstan has said. *I want you to teach me about the human heart.*

Dunstan.

Aris heads back downtown.

Bus Chatter

Old man: I'm going to see my daughter. She's gonna come back me to visit.

Driver: That's good. Been a while?

Old man: I didn't see her for fifteen years.

Driver: Wow. So it's a big day.

Old man: She told me to come. She wants me to see her kid.

Driver: Well, sit down, Grandpa, and I'll call out your stop.

This route hasn't changed much.

Aris notes the new display in the main lobby of the archives. She stores her bags in the locker and checks that her plastic ID is facing outward. As the elevator door is about to close she sees Bruce speeding by with a cart. He's dressed in a nice pair of pants and a light blue shirt. He has gotten taller or he has been lifting weights.

The door to the archives beckons.

The picture windows wave green limbs.

Aris goes to the desk for assistance.

Dunstan has been setting someone up at a terminal and when he turns and sees her there is a blip in the image, as if two films of Dunstan Regimbald have been spliced together. He doesn't acknowledge her until he is behind the desk.

Finger to glasses.

"Aris. Hello. How are you?"

Aris is blinded by the light from his face, even as he arranges information sheets and generally avoids looking directly at her.

"So you have a break coming? I have something for you down in my locker."

Dunstan is feeling the points of pencils, sorting those that need sharpening.

"Kind of busy right now."

"Really?" she stares at the pencils, "I'll wait."

He sighs and after talking to the woman in the office he steps around the desk and nods to her.

In the elevator down Aris resists the urge to remove a strand of wool from his vest.

"Keeping busy, I guess?" he half-heartedly says.

Aris smiles. "Everything's rolling along. The properties are on the market and I've given notice at my place."

"Good. That's good," he says.

Dunstan waits as Aris retrieves her jacket and bag from the locker.

"Let's go outside," she says.

They step out into an abnormally sunny day. The breeze takes the leaves and dust elsewhere. Aris heads for a bench and Dunstan follows.

Nice day," she says.

He doesn't reply.

"Okay," she says, a little irritated. "I bought you something."

Dunstan appears uncomfortable.

"You don't need to buy me anything. My job...."

"Oh, it's not for work done, Dunstan. You're good but not that good."

"Thank you very much," a glimmer of a smile.

"It's what you might call, or what I might call, an investment."

Aris opens her large tote and pulls out a paper bag.

"Here."

Dunstan reaches over, opens it and looks puzzled.

"Try it on."

He puts it on his head. Aris is reminded of drawings she did as a child, the sun with dark glasses and a drink with a straw, the moon with a night cap and a teddy bear in its moon hands.

"A hat," he says with the tentative voice Aris uses when she speaks French in public.

"Do I need a hat?"

Aris wants the confusion to end.

"Yes, Dunstan, you need a hat. You'll need it in Australia."

Confusion passes through the narrow inlet.

"Australia?"

And opens out into the sea.

"I want you to come with me. Come with me and find Maura Quell."

Dunstan takes the hat off and turns it slowly in his hands.

"Aris, I...."

She has been anticipating this. "The tickets are virtually paid for. Thank my moldering ex-husband and his zipper trouble. It's the perfect time to go. You'd have an easier time dealing with the institutions than I would. And if you're worried about the medical side, well, you could get the mega-checkup before you go. Get the best medical insurance. Derek will be happy to pay for it."

Is he embarrassed? Afraid?

"I'm not afraid," he corrects her thought.

She's prepared for all of this, for the equivocations.

"No."

Aris stares.

Dunstan puts the hat back in the bag.

"I'm sorry. Thank you, but no."

Her mind is sputtering.

"But, why not? Dunstan? This is a free trip. This is a chance, a great chance to get away. After all you've been through, don't you want a vacation?"

"No!"

He stands up, facing her.

"Look at me. Aris. After what I've been through, as you say.... Look, I don't want a vacation from my life."

He takes her face in his hands.

"I want a life."

And he walks away. Aris sits on the bench with her bag as the church nearby tolls its bloody bell.

It is hard, at first, to realize that she has been turned down by Dunstan Regimbald. Aris stands before the mirror that Cat Woman has promised to take when Aris leaves, and looks at her middle-aged frown, the crows' feet that look better on the crow, the gentle rolling hills of her body.

Dr. Grogan might say that she has hit the event horizon of her selfhood. Or a snag. She has finally caught up with herself, after all the running.

She remembered staring hard at her reflection when she was seven, and a tooth had come out. She remembered the fifteen year old vision, our lady of downcast eyes. And once in a store mirror after Derek departed, her green coat suddenly clown-like, all those tears in the Bay dressing room.

And now. Forty-seven. Forty-eight, forty-nine? Aris.

About to leave the continent with nothing in her hands.

Open-ended tickets are great for people like Aris. But the airlines are a mess, now, with advanced security, never mind the world fuel situation. They want to know her every move. They penalize changes of plan. God forbid she doesn't feel well the day of departure. Or her shoes have strangely-shaped Cuban heels. Or she carries along a water bottle. Or her meds are not in a clear plastic bag. God forbid she is less than Stalag about the whole thing.

She has arranged to take a hotel for the last few days in order to turn over the apartment and be done with it.

Seven years there. Seven winters watching the weather-stripping pull away from the balcony door. Seven years of extracting squashed up magazines from out of the tiny mailbox.

Aris knocks on the super's door and waits. When he opens it she sees a cat slink by the man's coffee table. Is she the only one that didn't take a kitten?

The turnover is simple. Here are your door keys, locker key, mailbox key.

"So, is it true you're going travelling?"

It would appear to be true.

Aris shakes the hand of the man she knows only as Mr. Henry and waits with her bags out front for her taxi.

The last days pass in a blur. Coffee shops, a novel she'd been saving for the flight. She makes sure her shoes are sound. She will need her shoes.

Sydney. Parramatta.

Just names in a book until now. Names on a map.

New South Wales.

"I want my map to come to life," Aris tells herself as she repacks her few things.

But all the way to the airport in the taxi she can't face it, the alone factor, as Dr. Grogan calls it.

Is she, like Maura, leaving everything she knows; is she as alone as that? Maura had thirteen years, and likely terrible circumstances, but Aris?

Maura would have had to be brave, standing in the courtroom of the Old Bailey, alone, a kid up against that wall of authority. How did she manage to get onto that boat?

Aris. Aris is a coward. She lets everything pass her by because she is afraid. All of the Aris Adventures—thank you, Dr. Grogan—are left untried. And in the end? She will die. The biggest adventure of them all. She will not be able to skip that one. And she'll lie there thinking of all the other ones she could have had, when her limbs were strong and her head was clear.

"I'm an idiot," she proclaims. The Pakistani taxi driver, it seems, would tacitly agree.

Check in. What is it now, a week ahead of the flight? Aris takes one last look at her bag as it makes its way along the belt. Soon she will have to enter the restricted area. There is little of interest there, so she wanders the main area, gleaning newspaper headlines. Apparently, there is a recession afoot. Or a global shift. A paradigm? A panic?

Aris buys a bag of *Cheetos.*

She can almost picture her parents waiting by the door as she headed out to her prom, her mother fussing with the pleats on the dress, her father looking a combination of elated and slain. And her grandmother looking up from the piano when Aris told her she'd been accepted at university.

Derek, avoiding her eyes as he packed.

Maura, looking back to the shore, seeing the bricks and stones of London, pretending her parents were in the fog by the dock, waving goodbye.

She is ready to go through security.

And that's when the light changes, cool silver light streams toward her.

"Aris."

Dunstan Regimbald, hat literally in hand, the man in the moon looking uncertainly at her.

"How the hell did you...?"

"Mr. Henry," he says. "He remembered what day you said you were leaving. Look, if I can't find which flights leave the city, how am I going to find her? That is, if the offer's still open."

Aris can't believe this. Uh...yes, but your ticket...."

"Never mind that." Dunstan produces a ticket in a folder. "I figured this was the only flight you'd be on today."

He says nothing else as they make their way through security. Shoes are removed, bags turned out. Aris wonders if they can see her artificial puppet heart thundering in her chest.

"Okay," she says when they are on the other side in no man's land.

"Turns out, I was afraid," he says before she can ask him. "And I'm tired of being afraid."

Aris feels something splinter inside.

"You know?" he asks.

She takes his hand.

He hesitates.

"It might take some time for all of my functions to return," he almost whispers.

Aris shakes his hand in hers. Is she laughing or crying?

"Mine, too," she says, and then they are both laughing, two people nobody wants to sit next to on an international flight, two people busy with papers, heads together as they pore over their little documents.

Failed academics, probably. Look at the pants on the guy. Look at the woman's sensible shoes.

"Do you think we'll find her? Aris asks. Their girl.

Aris and Dunstan hear their flight being called.

"We aren't sitting together," he says.

Aris takes his hand. "But we're going the same way."

They are leaving their shores. They are leaving all shores, soaring up into the sky. Aris looks down at the tiny city as they pull away.

📖

All the fingers of this hand. Who made it? Fingers to thumb, a star at the end of my hand.

We have seen a beast. Echidna. The boy tried to tell me all the names. Wallaby, echidna, platypus, kangaroo. Such names for such wayward animals as these, animals that wish to be other animals, or wish to be spirits, children playing at being animals, Eugene running through the forest, roaring and laughing. The beast was small and alone and left us to ourselves.

We took the horse and cart as far as we could, to the edge of the bush. It was so patient, standing and, I suppose, willing to wait forever. I unharnessed him and he stood there. It was maddening. I smacked him hard on the flank and he clopped away somewhere, not knowing he was free to go.

Mother, O, I tried.

There was food at some sort of shanty and nobody about. I entered and took dry cake and a pot of something stewed. I know I shouldn't steal, Mother. None of this should happen.

We ate back in the bush.

Caroline has yet to speak to me. I wish to know what has happened to her. I will tell her all my stories if she will tell me hers.

But she weakens. I try not to see it, but there is the dullness in her eyes. Light is passing from them. I have her by the hand, always, when we rest, and when we travel she leans on me.

We move slowly through this wilderness, so empty yet so full.

Mother, it is Eden, but a hard Eden.

Animals, trees that you would find so strange, and the sky at night! You could wish upon a thousand stars and keep on wishing.

Perhaps they will come after us. Perhaps they will leave us to this place. I don't suppose in the end I should mind. I am learning how to move among the roots and branches of this forest. It would catch up our Eugene, he would stumble, no doubt, but I can find my way.

I will not leave her.

Mother, I have left everyone in my life, or they have left me.

Her lips are cracked. Could a word escape them? Somewhere, I am sure, her parents are awaiting her return, just as you are waiting for me, Mother.

I will not leave her.

It is coming on dark. I find a hollow that offers some protection. Caroline's hair is a bird's nest. I smooth it and comb it through with my fingers, these mighty stars I wield.

I braid her hair.

Caroline, my twin, my friend.

See the stars at the ends of my hands? See what you've been given? A marvel entirely your own.

We will play at hide and seek, Caroline. We will hide and they will look for us. But we are very, very good. And I have always walked the woods. We will hide and they will seek, but we will win the game.

�֎

end

Acknowledgements

Any time a novel takes a writer on a journey of discovery there are always acknowledgements in its wake.

The online resources of the Old Bailey (London) were extremely inspiring, as were sites such as ancestry.ca and ancestry.uk. So much information is now available that one can find one's ancestors or, as a writer, create them. Individuals breathe through their temporal witness and testimony and somehow live beyond their time and place.

Other acknowledgements are also in order. Thanks to Reverend Bryan King for giving an itinerant writer a place to work. Thanks to my late agent, Frances Hanna, for believing in this book. She is missed in the Canadian literary world. Thanks as well to Bill Hanna for his steadfast hold of the reins at Acacia House, and for his expertise. Gratitude to John Buschek and BuschekBooks for giving Maura Quell a home. Thank you to family and friends who know when it is proper to ask, and not to ask, "How is the work going?"